October twenty-sixth marked Corinne's fifteenth birthday.

It fell on a Saturday. An afternoon at the beach, complete with a picnic supplied by Hally, was planned.

Two nights ago, Corinne had made the final payback of the money she had "borrowed" from the cookie jar. She had earned it by cleaning Hally's mother's studio and washing her car every week, in addition to baby-sitting the kids next door every Monday after school. She was also getting paid now for doing chores at home.

Mike owed it all to Hally. The woman was subtly, but inexorably becoming a major presence in their lives. A friend to his daughter. But *what* to him?

It was a question that lately had been robbing him of sleep. Right along with, What did he *want* her to be to him?

Dear Reader,

What a special lineup of love stories Silhouette Romance has for you this month. Bestselling author Sandra Steffen continues her BACHELOR GULCH miniseries with *Clayton's Made-Over Mrs.* And in *The Lawman's Legacy*, favorite author Phyllis Halldorson introduces a special promotion called MEN! Who says good men are hard to find?! Plus, we've got Julianna Morris's *Daddy Woke up Married*—our BUNDLES OF JOY selection—*Love, Marriage and Family 101* by Anne Peters, *The Scandalous Return of Jake Walker* by Myrna Mackenzie and *The Cowboy Who Broke the Mold* by Cathleen Galitz, who makes her Silhouette debut as one of our WOMEN TO WATCH.

I hope you enjoy all six of these wonderful novels. In fact, I'd love to get your thoughts on Silhouette Romance. If you'd like to share your comments about the Silhouette Romance line, please send a letter directly to my attention: Melissa Senate, Senior Editor, Silhouette Books, 300 E. 42nd St., 6th Floor, New York, NY 10017. I welcome all of your comments, and here are a few particulars I'd like to have your feedback on:
1) Why do you enjoy Silhouette Romance?
2) What types of stories would you like to see more of? Less of?
3) Do you have favorite authors?

Your thoughts about Romance are very important to me. After all, these books are for you! Again, I hope you enjoy our six novels this month—and that you'll write me with your thoughts.

Regards,

Melissa Senate
Senior Editor
Silhouette Books

Please address questions and book requests to:
Silhouette Reader Service
U.S.: 3010 Walden Ave., P.O. Box 1325, Buffalo, NY 14269
Canadian: P.O. Box 609, Fort Erie, Ont. L2A 5X3

LOVE, MARRIAGE AND FAMILY 101

Anne Peters

Silhouette

ROMANCE™

Published by Silhouette Books

America's Publisher of Contemporary Romance

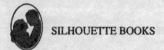

SILHOUETTE BOOKS

ISBN 0-373-19254-1

LOVE, MARRIAGE AND FAMILY 101

Printed in U.S.A.

Books by Anne Peters

Silhouette Romance

Through Thick and Thin #739
Next Stop: Marriage #803
And Daddy Makes Three #821
Storky Jones Is Back in Town #850
Nobody's Perfect #875
The Real Malloy #899
The Pursuit of Happiness #927
Accidental Dad #946
His Only Deception #995
McCullough's Bride #1031
*Green Card Wife #1104
*Stand-in Husband #1110
*Along Comes Baby #1116
My Baby, Your Son #1222
Love, Marriage and Family 101 #1254

Silhouette Desire

Like Wildfire #497

*First Comes Marriage

ANNE PETERS

shares her Pacific Northwest home with her husband, Manfred, and their aged dog, Adrienne. Anne treasures her family and friends, her private times, her creativity and, last but by no means least, her readers.

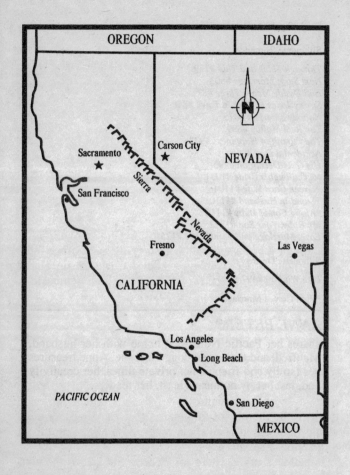

Chapter One

Mr. Michael John Parker was fifteen minutes late.

Through the glass partition of her so-called office—the only private office available—Halloran McKenzie glared at the large clock on the far wall of the school gymnasium, fingertips doing an impatient drumroll on her battered metal desk. It was her opinion that since she'd been accommodating enough to agree to a meeting after school hours, the least Corinne Parker's father could do was to show up on time.

It wasn't as if she didn't have plans of her own. This was the first day of her aerobics class and it was due to start in forty-five minutes. She owed it to her hips and thighs to be there. Not to mention that Garnet Bloomfield would think she'd once again reneged on her commitment to lose those saddlebags.

Impatience urged Hally to her feet. She paced the confines of her cubicle, thinking it was a good thing she'd at least had the foresight to change into her workout gear. This way she could be out of here and on her way the minute she was done laying down a few pertinent ground rules to the father of her truant young student. Provided he showed up within the next—*Hello!*

Hally's dark thoughts careened to a halt as, through the glass in her door, her eyes homed in on the man dodging the junior varsity basketball team's practice shots as he strode hurriedly toward her office in the back corner of the gym. *Well, well.*

If that was Mr. Parker—and who else would be bearing down on her office at this hour?—then he was everything she'd ever imagined a typical corporate army's top general to look like: grim-faced and pulled-up socks to the max.

In other words, precisely the kind of father most red-blooded teenagers would feel honor-bound to rebel against, not that that excused Corinne Parker's absences and chronic tardiness. It did throw some light, however, on the girl's penchant for grunge fashion and hacked-off bleached hair. No doubt she wanted to spite a father who expected his fourteen-year-old to wear pinafores and Mary Jane shoes.

Who should know better than she?

Hally pulled back from the glass a bit lest the man catch her watching his approach. She was appalled by the strength and instantaneousness of the antipathy she felt toward him, a man she'd never met. It had been years, after all, since she had been a rebellious fourteen-year-old with a father whose only resemblance to the man approaching her office lay in the sternly set facial expression, the immaculate business suit and flawless haircut.

All of which, admittedly, provided quite a startling contrast to the sweaty group of scruffy adolescents he was skirting with preoccupied grace and agility.

And to their coach, too.

Oh, for heaven's sake! Moving away from the door altogether, Hally impatiently chastised herself for that disloyal observation. After all, Gilbert Smith was her...well, "boyfriend" would do as well as anything else. And when he wasn't in ratty sweats and red as a beet from yelling at his team, Gil looked quite presentable, too. She on the other hand...

Hally glanced down at herself dressed in workout clothes and was suddenly irrationally self-conscious about her appearance. She wished she hadn't changed clothes, after all. More, she wished she already weighed five pounds less so that she wouldn't look as if she were stuffed into her leotard like a five-foot sausage into its casing. And though she scolded herself for these unprecedented and idiotic thoughts and feelings, she frantically cast around for something with which to cover as much of her less-than-perfect shape as possible.

She spotted a denim shirt and snatched it up. She had one arm in a sleeve when, after a cursory knock, the door opened.

"Ms. McKenzie?" It was the *GQ* cutout, of course. Entering at her distracted nod, he introduced himself. "Mike Parker. Sorry I'm late. Traffic...."

"That's all right." Struggling to appear composed, Hally fought to get her other arm into a maddeningly uncooperative garment.

"Here, let me..."

Mike Parker was helping her into the shirt with efficient courtesy before Hally could do more than stammer a flustered, "Th-thank you."

Up close, the man was physically even more imposing than he had seemed across the gym. He towered over her by a good head. Heat radiated from him—it had been ninety degrees out at noon and now it was certainly hotter. He smelled of clean male, starched linen and crisp aftershave. Hally stepped away from him the instant her shirt settled across her shoulders.

Excruciatingly aware of the glance with which he swept her leotarded frame, she retreated behind her desk and sat, all the while bemoaning her uncharacteristic lapse in professional appearance and demeanor. Ordinarily, given her lack of physical stature and—to her—terminally cute blondness, to establish credibility she always strove to dress and conduct herself with reserved dignity during first meetings such as this.

Very much afraid that in this case she had totally blown it, she tried to regain some lost ground with a cool smile and a hand gesture that silently invited her visitor to sit, as well.

He didn't. Instead he disconcerted her anew by ambling over to the pegboard wall to study her displayed diplomas. Well, let him, she thought, trying for unconcern. She had, after all, graduated with honors. And anyway, this meeting was about *him,* not *her.*

"Mr. Parker." Hally tightly folded her hands on the desk. Her posture was as erect as ever her mother could have wished it to be. "I'm afraid I have another appointment in a few minutes, so I'll come straight to the point. Your daughter Corinne…"

"Is lucky to have you for a teacher," her visitor disarmed her by interrupting. "If your credentials are anything to go by." He went to the chair and sat.

Not sure how to reply to this double-edged compliment, Hally looked down at her folded hands. Noting white-knuckled tension there, she willed herself to relax. She decided to forego a reply and to stick to the subject at hand.

"Corinne is a very troubled young woman," she said. She forced herself to levelly meet the man's eyes and was momentarily thrown off guard by the flicker of pain her words seemed to cause. It was masked so quickly by an expression of wary neutrality, however, that she decided she'd only imagined it in the first place.

Certainly his tone revealed nothing but skepticism as he said, "Isn't two weeks a bit soon to make that kind of sweeping assessment, Ms. McKenzie? After all, Cory is not only new to Ben Franklin High, being a freshman, but new to Long Beach, too. We only moved here a month ago.''

"I understand that," Hally said. "And believe me, I'm not the kind of teacher or counselor whose first course of action is a complaint to the student's parents."

"I have only your word for that, though, don't I?"

"No, Mr. Parker, you can check with the principal, too." Hally kept her tone pleasant but firm. Parker's bristling defensiveness, identical to every other parent's reaction to criticism of their child, was exactly what she'd needed to relax and regain a professional perspective. This was familiar ground and she trod upon it with confidence. "I've taught here at Ben Franklin for seven years—"

"This isn't about teaching, though, is it?" Michael Parker injected stiffly. "It's about you psychoanalyzing a student you barely know and—"

"Mr. Parker," Hally interrupted. She was not about to let him put her back on the defensive. "Quite aside from the fact that I do have a degree in psychology—"

"A *bachelor* degree," Mike Parker said dismissively. "With all due respect, Ms. McKenzie, they're a dime a dozen."

"Nevertheless." In spite of her resolve to remain unruffled, Hally began to seethe with resentment but didn't bother to point out to the man what he already knew very well from looking at her diplomas—namely her Masters in English. "I *have* taught school for seven years and I don't need to be a therapist to know that Corinne is having emotional problems *beyond* those related to a new environment."

Leaning forward, she drove home her point. "Are you aware, Mr. Parker, that out of the nine days school has been in session, your daughter has been absent four and tardy the rest?"

"Impossible." Betraying emotion at last, Parker surged

to his feet. "I personally drop her at the front steps of this school every morning. Let me see this."

Hally reflexively shrank back as he reached across the desk and snatched up Corinne's file. But though she had tensed to object to his high-handedness, she took a deep breath instead and held her tongue.

Let him see for himself the lengths to which a child will go to defy an overly controlling parent, she thought snidely.

And was ashamed of her pettiness the moment she saw the betrayed and thunderstruck expression with which the girl's father thumbed through the ream of obviously forged handwritten excuses in the file.

After several minutes of heavy silence, he muttered something harsh and succinct. He tossed the folder down on her desk. He turned away from Hally's gaze, one hand rubbing his mouth, the other clamped to the back of his neck. After a moment he dropped both hands with an audible sigh and the set of his shoulders lost some of its starch.

"I'm sorry," he said, flicking Hally a dark, sideways glance that, combined with the emotion-rough timbre of his voice, shook her up a lot more than it had any right to. "I had no idea...."

"I understand." Hally felt oddly self-conscious suddenly in the presence of this man's bewilderment and hurt, as if she'd trespassed on some private moment of grief. She felt bad, too, about her initial snap judgment of him. The unsettling resemblance she thought she had discerned between him and her father had long since been dispelled. She knew now that they were nothing alike. Mike Parker, whatever else he might or might not be, cared about this daughter. Whereas James McKenzie....

Well. Hally shook off the disturbing comparisons. Who knew? Feebly, she gestured to the phony excuses in the file. "Could anyone else have written these? A grand-mother, or—"

"No." Mike Parker went to his chair and heavily dropped into it. With his elbows propped on spread knees he bent his head and, his features taut with strain, stared fixedly at the fisted hand he cradled in his other.

Because they were extremely large hands, Hally stared at them, too. Raw-boned farmer's hands, they struck her as incongruous, sticking out as they did from the sleeves of an unmistakably hand-tailored suit. And they presented another difference between this man and her father whose hands were graceful and slim—the hands of a surgeon.

"Cory and I are alone, Ms. McKenzie."

"Yes..." It was in the file, of course. She glanced at his face. It was shuttered, devoid of emotion. Still, Hally's marshmallow heart went out to him even as her mind, after a quick glance at the clock, registered the fact she'd have to cut this conference short right now if she hoped to make her aerobics class on time.

But, of course, she wouldn't. Couldn't. They hadn't re-solved anything yet. She sighed. "I'm sorry."

"Yeah." His glance acknowledged her sympathy, but his tone made it clear he wouldn't welcome pity, in case that was offered, too.

It wouldn't have been. Mostly because Michael John Parker looked too tough in spite of his polish to be in need of it, or welcome it. His nose had clearly been broken at some point in his past and never been properly set, giving him the kind of face—interesting rather than handsome—that would draw second glances from men as well as from women. Second glances...but very little empathy.

Yet, Hally, though she fought against it, was filled with it. She'd always been a bleeding heart. "How long since..."

"A year." He spoke curtly, still staring at his hands. It

was obvious he didn't relish her questions and resented the necessity to answer them.

Hally sighed and stifled a need to apologize. After all, she wasn't idly prying, she was doing her job. Unfortunately for Michael Parker, it required that they communicate beyond the customary impersonal chitchat of strangers.

"Corinne is your only child?"

A mute nod confirmed what hadn't really been a question anyway. No siblings were listed in the records, and something about the girl's solitariness and oddly mature self-possession marked her an only child.

"And the two of you had no problems prior to your move to Long Beach?"

"I didn't say that."

"Then you did have problems?"

"Doesn't every family?" Mike looked up from his hands with a dark-eyed glare of resentment.

"Mr. Parker." Struggling for patience, Hally took a deep breath and quietly let it out. "I appreciate how difficult this must be for you..."

"Do you?"

"Well, y-yes...."

"How?"

"Well, I...." Thrown off balance, Hally momentarily faltered. Her earlier empathy waned in the face of his tight-lipped challenge. Affronted, she angled her chin. "Are you baiting me, Mr. Parker?"

"Not at all."

"Then what was the point..."

"The point, Ms. McKenzie, is that I very much doubt you can have any idea what it's like to lose your mate and suddenly find yourself on your own with an adolescent child you think you know but don't."

On his feet again, Mike paced the few steps of Hally's confined office space with the same agitation and pent-up violence her cat, Chaucer, displayed in his carrier during trips to the vet.

"I'm at my wits' end here, Ms. McKenzie." Parker's tone was low, but fierce. "And what I need from you is *help*, not simpering platitudes about knowing how I feel."

He grabbed the edge of the desk and pinned her to her seat with his eyes. "You don't know squat about how I feel."

"I know that you're angry and that it has nothing to do with me," Hally said steadily. The flare of alarm she'd initially felt at his outburst had been only that—a flare, as quickly extinguished as ignited by the recognition that frustration, not violence, had driven him to it. "And I'm quite convinced now that you care about Corinne..."

"You doubted that?" He pulled back, his tone as incredulous as his expression.

Hally shrugged. "Corinne is a new student with—you'll excuse my bluntness—nothing much to recommend her so far. And you..."

"What about me?"

"Well, to be frank, everything about you shouts 'upwardly mobile executive,' which leads me to wonder just how much of your time you can spare to hands-on parenting."

"I can *spare* as much time as it takes," Mike growled, furious at the implication of parental neglect when he'd been knocking himself out trying to do the right things. "But I do have to make a living, I can't be in two places at once, and until *you* finally did your job and notified me, *I* had no way of knowing that my daughter wasn't in school when she was supposed to be. Now did I?"

His eyes drilled into her, daring her to refute his logic. Hally couldn't, but that didn't mean she was prepared to back down. She stared at him with all the authority she could muster and waited in silence until he sat down.

"Thank you," she said coolly, much as she would say

to one of her students after she'd subjugated them with one of her looks.

So secretly—and unprofessionally—thrilled was she with this minor victory over the formidable Michael J. Parker that she forgot all about the extra inch on her thighs and the fact that her tights offered nothing in the way of camouflage.

She shoved her chair back from her desk and crossed her legs. "Now that that's out of the way," she said briskly, "let's discuss how the situation should be handled...."

Troubled and pensive, Mike slowly traversed the now-deserted school parking lot on his way to his car. Strange woman, that Halloran McKenzie, he thought. Talk about contradictions—the mind of Dr. Joyce Brothers in Shirley Temple's head and Marilyn Monroe's body. Combined, those traits made for a very tantalizing package, however, he had to admit. And he doubted many boys missed her English class.

This somewhat wry reflection abruptly recalled him to his troubles since it reminded him that his daughter evidently did miss English and every other class with frightening regularity.

Grimly, he started the car and pulled out into traffic, knowing he would have to have a serious talk with Cory when he got home. He dreaded it. It seemed not a day went by that they weren't at each other over *something*. And, man, he was tired of it. In fact, he was tired period. Being mom and pop, housekeeper, breadwinner and disciplinarian to a recalcitrant teenager was wearing him out.

Cruising the route home on automatic pilot, and removed by time and distance from the dedicated Ms. McKenzie's ardently persuasive plea for patience, Mike thought that giving in to Cory's demands just might be the best thing to do after all.

Why *not* let her go back home? Why not let her go back to Idaho, to Marble Ridge, to Becky's folks? Lord knew they were at him about it almost as much as Corinne was, if for different reasons. Cory professed to hate him, whereas the Campbells simply didn't deem any man alone capable of raising a teenage daughter.

And maybe that was why he wasn't letting Cory go— because his in-laws were right and, aside from the fact that he didn't much care to be pressured, he needed to prove them wrong.

Mike knew that wasn't really the reason he had so far hung tough, though. Part of it, sure. But another part was that, while alive, his wife had clung way too tightly to her parents, and even to his, only three miles further down the road. Becky's dependence had given the older folks the impression they could butt in whenever they felt like it, an attitude that didn't fly with Mike at all.

But even that wasn't the main reason for his determination to bring up his daughter himself from here on in. That had strictly to do with himself and Cory. She was *his* daughter, *his* child. She was the baby he and Becky had been so happy to have created. And she'd grown to be a stranger.

His fault. Drilling for oil all over the globe didn't leave a man with much family time. Nor was three weeks of home leave every four months anywhere near enough time for a father to bond with his child. A child who didn't understand why he wasn't around like other daddies; who considered his long absences a form of desertion no matter how often he tried to explain the real reason for their lifestyle.

Not that he hadn't understood Cory's bewilderment and agonized over her increasingly resentful attitude. After all, what could something as intangible as the dream of a horse ranch possibly mean to a young child? Or for that matter, to anyone other than Becky and himself?

It was *their* dream. Just as it had been *their* decision to live as they had—he overseas in his oil camps, Becky home with Corinne in Marble Ridge—to one day make that dream a reality.

Where else could a geologist earn the kind of money Mike had brought home than in those faraway oil fields? Money a fair chunk of which they had faithfully put into savings each month. Watching it grow—every dime and dollar reducing by minutes and hours the time they'd have to wait to be a family again—was what had made it all bearable.

And then, just like that, time had run out.

First, Becky had become strange and secretive, increasingly so. And then her illness had taken its toll, draining their savings account as relentlessly as the cancer had sucked the life from her body. And their dream had collapsed like a house of cards in a windstorm with Becky's death.

Cory's grief had been as terrible as his own bewilderment. He couldn't seem to figure out how everything could have gone so wrong. And while the loss should have drawn them closer, it had, instead, driven them further apart.

Cory had been livid, wild, out of control with rage when she'd seen him packing to fly back to Saudi three days after the funeral. She didn't want anything to do with him, was more than happy to live with her maternal grandparents, but she was nevertheless outraged that he was leaving.

Nothing he or Becky's parents could say had been able to make her understand the necessity. She didn't care about Mike's unbreakable contract, didn't want to hear that they were practically bankrupt, or that the sizable sum he'd earn in the next six months would allow him to take another position with his company for less pay and with virtually no travel.

That was the position he now held here in Long Beach, California. A town that, in many ways, was as far removed from Marble Ridge, Idaho, as the moon. But even so, it was a community in which Mike had hoped to make a new beginning for himself and his child. To make up for lost time. To become a family.

So far, their month here together had been a disaster.

Sighing, Mike pulled into the lot of the supermarket he'd come to know better than he ever thought he'd have to. Grocery shopping was just one of the many new dimensions to his life.

Pushing his cart up and down the aisles, he hoped to spot the items they were out of since he'd forgotten—again—to bring the list he'd made that morning. Cruising the aisles wasn't the most efficient way to shop, but what the heck.

He detoured abruptly when he spotted the by-now-familiar—and dreaded—redhead who lived two doors down from him. A forty-ish and still quite attractive divorcée, Pamela Swigert had been the first to welcome Corinne and him into the neighborhood. She had two children, both of whom had names Mike considered as strange and outlandish as their mother's flamboyant wardrobe. The daughter, Latisha, was Corinne's age, while the poor kid named Warlock was twelve.

Latisha didn't go to Corinne's school, but the two girls had struck up a desultory friendship of sorts. Though not sure how or whether to discourage the association of these two vastly dissimilar girls, Mike was nevertheless uneasy about the changes Cory's appearance had undergone with Latisha's tutelage. Instead of the preppy, brown-haired young girl from Idaho who favored Laura Ashley, Corinne now dressed in Goodwill castoffs and had bleached her chopped-off hair a sickly white.

As to Pamela Swigert, upon learning that there was no Mrs. Parker, she had taken to unexpectedly dropping in with offerings of food and parenting advice, neither of which Mike particularly appreciated any more than the flirty come-hither attitude that accompanied them.

He had neither the time nor the inclination to enter into any kind of romantic liaison with a woman, *any* woman. But most certainly not with a neighbor, even if she had been his type, which Pam decidedly was not. Trouble was, he had no idea how to let her know that without hurting her feelings.

Which was why Mike chose avoidance whenever possible, inconvenient though that was. Like right now, with Pam Swigert in the frozen food section where Mike needed to get some things, as well. A pizza, for one thing. It was Cory's favorite food and Mike figured if they shared one for dinner, the talk they were going to have to have just might go a little easier. Hell, he'd get her Rocky Road ice cream, too. As soon as the coast was clear.

Mike backed up a few steps and peered around the corner. And stifled an oath when he found himself practically nose to nose with a delighted Pamela Swigert.

"Mike!" she exclaimed, fluttering night-black eyelashes that never failed to fascinate Mike, they were so impossibly thick and long. *False,* Corinne had scornfully proclaimed them. "I thought that was you I saw skulking by a minute ago."

She tapped him on the arm with a flirty moue. "Not trying to avoid me, were you?"

"Lord no." Mike mustered a grin. "Just a bit preoccupied, I guess."

"Problems?" Pam was instantly all sympathetic concern. "Anything I can do?"

"Oh, no." *Heaven forbid.* To change the subject, Mike craned his neck to look past her. "This the frozen food aisle?" he asked, as if he didn't know. "Thought I'd get us a pizza—"

"Pizza?" Pam squealed, pointing to the two large

rounds in her own cart. "Can you beat that! Great minds do think alike, I swear. I've got enough here for you to join Warly and me. It'll be fun.

"Come on," she insisted prettily, gripping his arm when Mike pulled back, ready to say no. "Don't be a poop."

A "poop"? Mike shook his head, chuckling a little rue-fully as he gently but firmly peeled Pam's fingers off his arm. Sparkly little hearts on her inch-long, deep red nails momentarily arrested his gaze before he lifted it to her skillfully made-up face.

"Thanks for the invite, Pamela," he said. "But I'm afraid it's just not a good time for us to be sociable right now...."

Pam's smile remained in place, but one pencil-sharp eyebrow arched. "Since by 'us' you obviously mean your-self and Corinne, dear heart, I suppose that means you don't know after all."

"Don't know what?" Anxiety slammed into Mike's gut like a boxer's fist.

Pamela's light laugh held an edge of uneasiness. "About the rock concert at Milton Stadium. I dropped the girls off there half an hour ago."

"What?" Mike had to hold on to his cart with both hands to keep himself from grabbing the woman and shak-ing her till her capped teeth rattled. "You took Corinne to a rock concert without my permission?"

Faced with his barely leashed fury, Pamela blanched. "W-well," she stammered before gathering herself to-gether with a flare of indignation. "I thought she *had* your permission."

"Did she say she did?"

"Not in so many words, no." Pam tossed her glossy mane with obvious pique. "But she certainly had the money."

"Money?" Just that morning Corinne had demanded her allowance—fifteen dollars—because she was broke.

Mike had told her she'd get it as soon as she did her chores.

"How much money?" Mike asked, sickness gathering in the pit of his stomach.

"She had a fifty-dollar bill."

She had a fifty-dollar bill. Letting himself into the house, Mike was still reeling from that statement and its implications. His daughter was no longer just a rebel at odds with herself, her father and her circumstances, she was a thief. A *thief!*

Thunderstruck, Mike had abandoned his grocery cart and walked out of the store without another word to the visibly shaken Pamela.

Dropping onto a chair at the kitchen table where a cereal box and two milky bowls bespoke this morning's hasty departure, he felt as if he had taken a beating—defeated and sore right down to his bones. He felt so deeply and utterly betrayed that he would have wept had he had the tears.

Putting his elbows on the table, he dug his fingers into his scalp and despaired of ever being able to reach his daughter after this.

What had the teacher said after he'd spelled out to her how things were between Corinne and him?

"Time, patience and love, Mr. Parker. That's what your daughter needs from you right now. Except for the basics such as pulling her weight around the house, leave the rules and the discipline to me here at school for the time being...."

So how do you propose I handle this, *Ms. McKenzie?*

Mike raised his head. He looked around the cozy kitchen, his eyes flicking over each familiar item they'd brought with them from Idaho as if he'd never seen any of it before. His gaze stopped at the white porcelain cat with its slightly chipped, raised black paw.

It was Becky's cookie jar, which now served as the bank
for the emergency cash he liked to keep around the house.
A couple of hundred dollars, for those unexpected inci-
dentals. It was a carry-over from his parental home, and
probably no longer even necessary in this day of credit
cards and ATMs.

Slowly, his eyes never leaving the silly cat, Mike rose
from his chair and walked over to the shelf on which it
sat. He stood in front of it for a long time, staring at it and
debating with himself whether he really wanted to do this
or not. He leaned heavily toward *not*. There really was a
certain comfort in not knowing the truth.

Coward? No.

Jaw set, Mike grabbed the jar. Putting one hand on one
of the cat's ears, he raised the lid. He set lid and jar down
on the counter and reached inside. Irrationally, his heart
lifted a little as his fingers latched onto several bills. As if
having Cory steal from strangers was better than having
her steal from him. He pulled the bills out. There were
four of them. He fanned them a little. Three twenties and
a ten.

His chin dropping to his chest, Mike closed his fist
around the bills, crumpling them. A sound very much like
a dry sob rose into his throat and refused to be swallowed.
It burst from him with terrible force as he blindly stared
at the crumpled bills in his hand and raggedly exhaled.

In all, the bank was short one hundred and thirty dollars.

Chapter Two

It was well past six o'clock when Hally pulled her classic, buttercup yellow convertible VW Bug into the drive on her side of the duplex she co-owned with her mother. The house was a white stucco affair, pre-World War II, and each half had its own sweep of wide steps leading up to its own pillared veranda and its own front door. A lawn hardly bigger than a place mat separated the two sets of steps that were each flanked by flowering shrubs.

A one-car garage sat back from each side of the house at the end of the respective driveways, but neither Hally nor her mother used the squat little building for its designated purpose. For Hally it served as a catch-all storage place while Edith Halloran McKenzie had converted the garage into a studio in which she created her fabulous stained-glass art.

Hally could hear the telephone through her screened open windows as she unlocked her front door. Hurrying inside, she tripped over Chaucer who, as usual, appeared out of nowhere and was trying to beat her into the house.

The cat yowled his indignant protest, drowning out Hally's muttered epithet. In the kitchen, she lunged for the phone just as its ring abruptly stopped.

Garnet Bloomfield, she thought with a baleful glare at the instrument. With a sigh of vexation, she plunked her bulging tote on the nearest chair and her keys on the kitchen table. *Probably called to read me the riot act for not showing up for aerobics.*

As if I had a choice.

Out of sorts, Hally bent and absently stroked Chaucer who was winding himself around and between her legs in a bid for apology and attention. She fretted. The meeting with Michael J. Parker had been necessary but, darn it—this new school year was supposed to be the beginning of a whole new chapter in her life. Her horoscope had said as much. Her bank account agreed—come June it was time to cut loose and make a change.

Which meant that come June she would pack her bags, lease out the house and hit the road to Florence, Italy, for the year-long sabbatical that had always been her dream. Or, if not always, at least since a certain medical student had cured her of romance back in college.

Before the trip began, however, she planned to be a whole different person. For one thing, she intended to have a leaner body. And long, smooth tresses that could be swept back into a simple and classic hairstyle. She also meant to acquire the kind of simple and classic wardrobe in basic black, taupe and cream that never went out of style. Especially in Europe.

"I'm gonna have to get tougher with my time, Chauce," she muttered, and puffed out another long breath of vexation as she straightened. Today's aerobics class was to have been step one on the road to *Fiorenze*. Tomorrow night's Italian language class would be step two.

"And nothing's darn well going to interfere with that," Hally emphatically informed the cat. Living alone, conversations with Chaucer were a normal occurrence. "I've waited too long for this to let myself get sidetracked by other people's problems.

"Oh, all right." Giving in to the cat's insistent pleas, Hally grabbed a can of cat food out of the cupboard, opened it and dumped it into a bowl. "If you aren't going to listen, you might as well eat." She set the food on the floor. "Here. Stop complaining."

As Chaucer fell on his meal as if he hadn't had nourishment in years, Hally filled another dish with water, set it on the floor, as well, and flicked on the radio.

"Police used tear gas and water hoses to subdue hundreds of rioting teenagers at Milton Stadium where the Leapin' Lizards, a popular rock group, unexpectedly canceled their scheduled appearance...."

Horrified by what she was hearing, Hally stood frozen at the sink. Teakettle in hand, she stared at the radio. Almost certainly some of the kids involved or affected by the mob scene would be students of hers.

"One death and scores of injuries are reported. Details in—"

Hally didn't wait to hear more. Her resolution of nonextracurricular involvement forgotten, she had already scooped up her keys and was out the door.

It was not very far from her house to the stadium, a couple of dozen blocks. Hally broke several traffic laws on her way over, ignoring stop signs and speed limits alike. A sense of urgency spurred her on; she couldn't shake the feeling that she was needed at the site.

Pandemonium reigned on the street in front of the stadium. Hally got out of her car several blocks away and ran the rest of the way on foot. Patrol cars, lights flashing like psychedelic beacons, formed a four-direction barrier around the milling crowd that was surrounded by officers in riot gear. Several ambulances with rotating lights like glaring strobes were inside the parameter. The air smelled of sulfur and hovered like rancid fog over the nightmare scene. The noise was incredible—shrill, desperate and angry human voices trying to make themselves heard over sobs, screams and curses punctuated by sirens, and the thud of nightsticks connecting with the backs of those who still dared rebel.

Hally pushed and elbowed her way through the volatile crowd of spectators, parents and freaked-out kids who surged against—and were barely held back by—the human bulwark of the riot police. She didn't know whom she was looking for. No one in particular she would have said, if asked. She only knew she had to be here, to be available to help in case—

When she suddenly saw Mike Parker, grim-faced and ashen, at the far edge of the crowd, the realization that she'd come here looking for *him* smacked her in the face like a stinging slap. *Oh, no-oo…*

Appalled, she tried to spin on her heel and run the other way. Hemmed in by the crowd, however, this was impossible. She did the next best thing and sharply averted her face, though not before noting with a pang that the man seemed to have aged ten years since leaving her office less than two hours ago. And that his formerly immaculate hair was a mess of rumpled waves, his suit jacket hung open, and his loosened tie was askew. He looked like he'd been through the wringer.

Because all of her nobler instincts urged her to rush to him and offer assistance, Hally fought desperately to stay where she was. Face contorted from battling herself as much as from the jabs, shoves and pushes the milling crowd was inflicting, she sternly reminded herself that what Michael Parker and his daughter needed was more than she was willing to give. She had her own agenda, her own plans and goals, and they didn't include a troublesome widower with an even more troublesome daughter. She had given him the best professional advice she could.

Oh, damn! She gasped as a sharp elbow stabbed into

her ribs and heels ground down on her instep. She swiveled around and once again caught sight of Mike Parker. He looked lost and terribly alone as he scanned the crowd for a glimpse of his daughter.

"Michael!" Hally yelled, the name erupting from her without conscious will. Realizing that there was no way he could hear her, she shoved and strong-armed her way toward him. "Mr. Parker!" It was like fighting an incoming tide. Worse, it was like one continuous series of head-on collisions that soon left her battered and breathless.

And yet she fought on, drawn by *something* from this man she barely knew, and resenting it every step of the way. Still, she continued to yell his name, continued to wave one arm above her head while pushing forward with the other.

And all the while calling herself every kind of a fool.

When Mike finally became aware of her struggle toward him, for one brief instant the terrible strain and anguish that marred his face eased into something like gladness and relief.

Hally felt an answering gladness inside of herself, which she instantly squelched with a stern, *You'll help him find his daughter and that's all.* She watched him move in her direction, using his superior height and visible determination to meet her halfway.

He had almost reached her when something hard smacked Hally right between the shoulder blades at the same time as her legs got tangled up with someone else's. She lost her footing and her breath simultaneously. She stumbled and fell to her knees, and the sea of humanity closed in around her. She tried to get back on her feet. Couldn't. Couldn't get up, couldn't breathe. Feet stepped on her, bumped her. She screamed.

"Halloran! Halloran McKenzie!"

Hally could hear Mike Parker's voice, but blackness was closing in. She was being smothered, trampled. *Help!*

"Oh, God. There you are." Strong hands hauled Hally to her feet, supported her as she swayed, gasping for air. "Are you all right?"

Hally blinked back the fog clouding her vision. Her ears rang. Mike Parker's worried face wove in and out in a dizzying pattern. She choked back a wave of nausea and dug her nails into his sleeves. "I'm f-fine..."

"I doubt it," she saw as much as heard Mike say before he half dragged, half carried her to the edge of the crowd. Like a distant observer she was aware of him wiping dirt off her face and smoothing down her clothes. His ungainly hands were incredibly gentle.

The moment that registered, Hally stepped away from him with a choked, "Thanks."

Mike's hands dropped to his sides, closed into fists. "What're you doing here?" His face was gray. "You could've been killed."

"Yes, well." Gradually the world slid back into focus and Hally was able to meet Mike's bleak, searching gaze. She ran a shaky hand through her short crop of curls. She cleared her throat.

"C-Corinne?" she croaked.

If possible, Mike's face grew grayer still. "All I know is that she's here. Somewhere..."

"I was afraid of that."

For just an instant they stared into each other's eyes and recognized an emotional connectedness that neither would have consciously welcomed or acknowledged. It was gone with the flick of a lash as Hally heard the frantic call of her name.

"Ms. McKenzie! Ms. McKenzie!"

She looked around and spotted another woman in the thick of things. She was waving her hands and bobbing up and down like a cork in the sea some fifteen feet away. Hally recognized her as the parent of one of her former, as well as present students.

"Mrs. Undser!"

"Have you seen Susan?" the woman shouted as the jostling crowd dragged her in a direction away from Hally and Mike.

Hally shook her head, hard. "No. But I'll keep an eye out for her, okay?"

The woman's answering nod was distracted. She was fighting against the current of humanity just as Hally had been.

"Look." Mike's fingers bit into Hally's arm and reclaimed her attention. "Over there. Corinne."

Hally swiveled her head in the direction he pointed. Sure enough, Corinne Parker's spiky bleached hair surfaced for a moment in the sea of restlessly milling youngsters the police had cordoned off.

"Come on." Grabbing Hally's hand, Mike shoved toward the line of patrolmen with aggressive purpose.

Hally used her own free arm and hand to help him clear a path. "They're herding her into that police van over there!" she yelled, needlessly, since Mike could certainly see what was happening, too.

"Officer." They had reached the armored human wall around the kids. "Please," Mike implored the nearest policeman. "I've got to get through. That's my daughter over there. She's only fourteen, an innocent bystander. I know she didn't do anything."

Except steal from me.

"Move along, sir," the beleaguered lawman said curtly.

"But she didn't do anything!" Mike repeated with angry exasperation. "If you'll just let me go and get her..."

"I'm telling you only once more," the officer bellowed. "Move along. They're all innocent to hear them tell it."

The officer glared at Mike, brandishing his nightstick. "Move now. Get."

"Come on, Mike." Hally tugged on Mike's arm to end

the glaring contest she knew Mike had no chance of winning. The policeman held all the cards.

"Where are they taking the kids?" she asked the patrolman.

"Downtown."

"Come on." Hally pulled the fuming and reluctant-to-capitulate Mike forcibly away.

"There's nothing you can accomplish here," she told him across her shoulder. "But at least you can be at the other end to bail her out. Where's your car?"

"Don't have it," Mike said grimly.

Hally frowned at him. "Then how…"

"Got a ride from a neighbor." Mike clenched his teeth, rage consuming him. Damn that stiff-necked policeman. And damn Pam Swigert for getting Corinne into this mess in the first place. He didn't care that it wasn't entirely fair to blame the woman, any more than he cared to admit that this stranger his daughter had become would have found a way to get here, no matter what. He needed to blame someone—anyone.

And for the moment he was too overwrought to concede that the only one he should be blaming was himself.

"Where is he?" Hally asked, meaning the neighbor.

"She," Mike absently corrected, frowning as he looked around. He had only just become aware that Pam had become separated from him somewhere along the line. "I don't know. She's a redhead…"

He scanned the crowd, concerned now for his neighbor's well-being in spite of his anger. What if Pamela had fallen and been trampled, like Halloran McKenzie had nearly been? This was no place for anyone alone, least of all a woman.

"Is that her?" Hally pointed, already moving that way.

Mike followed. "Yes." Alarm slammed into him. Pam was surrounded by several other women. She was crying. Black rivulets ran down her cheeks. Her always perfectly coiffed hair looked like a swarm of birds had gotten tangled up in it. She was obviously in great distress. "Pamela!"

He surged toward her, Hally in tow. "For God's sake, what happened?" He let go of Hally to take hold of and support his distraught neighbor instead.

"Some kids beat on her pretty good," one of the other women said when Pam just wailed and buried her face against Mike's chest.

"Take me home," she cried, blindly reaching out with one hand. To Mike's shock and surprise, Latisha was there to take it. Corinne's so-called friend.

Rage overcame him once more. "Why aren't you with Cory?" he shouted at the hapless girl who, he only then noticed, was sobbing and as disheveled as her mother.

"W-we g-got se-separated and...and...."

"Never mind," Mike said tiredly, his anger gone as abruptly as it had been aroused. It was all such a mess, such total madness. And there was nothing to be gained by yelling and carrying on.

"Halloran..." Guiding Pamela and her daughter out of the melee, he turned to Hally. "Look, I've got to drive them home. Could you... I mean, I know it's an imposition, but could..."

"I go to the police station and find Corinne?" Hally finished for him when he hesitated. And as everything inside her yelled, *No, no, no,* she heard herself say, "Sure. Though you realize I won't be able to spring her."

"I know. I'll get there myself just as quickly as I can. And, Halloran—" He gripped Hally's shoulder and stopped her as, with a quick nod, she started to move away to go to her car. "Thanks."

"Sure," Hally said, averting her eyes because the weary gratitude in his was making her feel like a phony. The last thing she wanted to do was to go to that police station.

She moved away from Mike's touch, thinking, How do I get myself into these things?

It smelled of dust, sweat and unwashed humanity. People were everywhere. Some clean, some not so. Some drunk. All of them unhappy to be there, even the police officers on duty, it seemed to Mike. Certainly they had long since given up on cordiality or even professional courtesy.

Tempers were short on both sides of the counter.

As promised, Hally was there, waiting for him. She had ascertained that the van carrying the adolescent miscreants had arrived and that the kids were being held in one large cell at the back of the building.

Irate parents were demanding the release of their offspring, Mike included. Harried officers were wrestling with the paperwork that would allow them to let go of their unwanted guests in the back, and thus clear the station of the throng of outraged citizens in the front.

Conversation between Mike and Hally was sparse as they waited for Corinne to be escorted out. At odd moments throughout the drive home with Pam, on the subsequent drive home in his own car over to the station, and even during his dealings with the law, Mike would recall that he wasn't alone in this fight for and with his daughter, and he'd experience a sense of wonder that left him puzzled and discomfited. And not a little scared.

Scared because Halloran McKenzie was the first woman since Becky who'd stirred in him a desire to know her better. A whole lot better.

Which, of course, simply could not be. He had enough on his plate without adding the complications of a romantic fling. If he knew what was good for him, he'd best get things back on a strictly professional footing right away.

"Ms. McKenzie." Taking a deep breath, he slanted her a strained smile. "I don't know how to thank you."

"Then don't," Hally said. She was tired and also a bit put off by the waves of reserve now emanating from this brooding man like chilled air from an open refrigerator. She spoke curtly. "I'm heading home, but I expect to see Corinne in my office a half hour before class tomorrow morning."

"I'll see to it," Mike promised, uncomfortably aware that he had affronted her, but in no condition, emotionally, to try to rectify the situation even if he wanted to. Which he didn't.

The woman was his daughter's teacher and assigned counselor. It was in the latter capacity that she had rushed to the stadium, looking to help. It had not been him personally she had aided out there, or even here at the station—it was the parent of one of her charges.

As she spoke to him, her face, smudged with dirt and lined with fatigue, was stern. And her tone was cool and professional.

"As we agreed," she said, "I'd like you to pick Corinne up *from* school as well as drive her *to* school for the next several days, just to let her know we're working in concert and that tabs are being kept. Please understand, however, that my interest can, of necessity, not go beyond her performance at school. I've got nine other students to counsel and I'd be a nervous wreck if I got personally involved in their home situations beyond what pertains to their studies. You do see that?"

"Absolutely," Mike said, telling himself that was exactly what he wanted from her and no more. "Our family problems have nothing to do with you."

"Well, at least not directly. So—" Hally shoved back her hair and met his eyes "—I'll say good-night then."

"G'night." Mike half raised his hand as she backed away from him toward the exit. "Thanks again."

Out on the sidewalk Hally congratulated herself on having made her position clear. Having done her good deed for the day, she told herself, she could now get on with her life. Future contact with Mike Parker would be minimal, confined to her office and school hours.

Bone-weary and longing for a bath, she stuck the key in the driver's side door of her car. Turning it, her gaze slid down and sideways, past the front wheel to the pavement. Only to snap right back to the front tire with a gasp of dismay. It was flat. The darned tire was flat!

What next? Momentarily overcome by what was definitely the last straw, Hally let her forehead drop to the roof of the car.

What have I done to deserve this? she questioned whatever unkind fate had decreed she shouldn't go home just yet. I'm tired, I'm hungry....

"Ms. McKenzie?"

Hally's head jerked up. She took a deep breath and slowly turned around. In front of her, looking concerned, stood Mike Parker. And next to him, managing to look both truculent and defiant, stood Corinne.

"What's the matter?" Mike asked, frowning. "What happened?"

As Hally wordlessly pointed; her gaze remained on her student. "Are you all right, Corinne?"

The girl gave a careless shrug and looked away, lips set in a stubborn line. But something had flickered in her eyes before she had averted them, and now she visibly swallowed.

She's not as tough as she wants us to believe, Hally thought.

And knew with a kind of sinking feeling that all the rhetoric she had spouted earlier to Mike and herself about not getting personally involved had likely been just that— rhetoric. Looking at the girl, involvement seemed somehow inevitable.

As it usually had been in at least one case, with at least

one student, every year for as long as Hally had been teaching.

Maybe it was because she could have used a sympathetic counselor herself when she was young and lost and so terribly at odds with the world. Her mother, dear friend that she since had become, had at the time been too miserable in her crumbling marriage herself to have been much support to her bewildered and unhappy younger daughter.

Whatever, some kids simply struck a chord; kids who needed understanding and support above and beyond the job description. Corinne Parker was one of those kids.

And it had nothing to do with the girl's father.

To underscore that, Hally replied brusquely to Mike's offer of help. "You get your child home, Mr. Parker. I've changed tires before, thank you very much."

Ignoring his taken-aback expression, she bid both of the Parkers good-night and went to get the jack, wrench and spare tire out of her trunk.

Only to be elbowed aside, and not very gently. "I'd appreciate it, Ms. McKenzie," Mike said without making a secret of the fact that it cost him to approach her after her outright rebuff, "if you'd have a word with Cory while I tend to this. She refuses to speak to me.

"And, yes..." He grimly forestalled the protest he was sure Hally was about to make. "I do realize that my request exceeds the boundaries you established, but—"

"I wasn't going to refuse," Hally interrupted, not bothering to argue any longer with him about the tire he was wrestling out of the trunk. "If you'll hand me your keys and point out which car is yours, Corinne and I will go sit in it."

"It's the Buick," Mike said, handing her the keys. "Seems like I owe you thanks all over again."

"No, you don't," Hally said. "I haven't done anything yet."

She walked away, but she did hear Mike mutter, "That's where you're wrong."

Not sure what to make of that, she touched the girl's slumped shoulder, making her jump. "Come on, Corinne. Let's go sit in your dad's car."

"While he fixes your tire?"

"That's right."

"I thought you knew how to do that yourself?" the girl muttered sullenly, keeping her eyes on the ground as she shuffled along at Hally's light prod in the back.

"I do," Hally said calmly. Sullen lippiness was something she could handle. Most kids resorted to that as their first line of defense. "But I wanted to talk to you."

"You mean, *he* wanted you to talk to me," Corinne sneered with a baleful glance at her father, hunkered down by the front wheel of the VW Bug.

"Yes, he did." Hally unlocked the door of the late-model Buick that Mike had indicated was his. It was her policy to be strictly honest with her students. No games, no subterfuge, no secret pact with their parents. And she expected complete honesty from them in return.

"Get in." Sliding in behind the wheel, she reached over and unlocked the passenger door.

She watched with weary amusement as Corinne plunked herself down on the seat with a put-upon air. It was hot in the car and, like Hally, she left her door ajar. Slouching, she looked down at her hands. In profile, with traces of baby fat still rounding the contours of her face, she looked achingly vulnerable and oh, so young.

"Were you one of the rioters?" Hally asked. The outright question startled some life into the girl. She turned her head and blinked at Hally.

But her answer was predictably rude. "So what if I was?"

Hally regarded her calmly. Her gaze held the girl's, who

clearly wanted to look away. "Did you know that someone was killed there tonight?"

Corinne visibly swallowed. She sucked her lips inward. Her lashes fluttered and Hally saw a sudden sheen of tears glaze her eyes before she turned her face aside.

Hally's voice softened. "Now, do you really want your father and me to think that you had a part in that?"

Looking down, the girl gave her head a quick, negative jerk.

"I didn't think so." Hally reached out to give Corinne's hand a reassuring pat. It was instantly jerked away.

Hally ignored the rebuff. In truth, it was no more than she had expected. "I want to help," she said, "if you'll let me."

"Humph."

"Your father is not the enemy, you know," Hally said quietly. And was startled in spite of herself by Corinne's vehement and venomous retort.

"He hates me." The girl's face twisted into an ugly mask of anguish and disdain. As if sensing that Mike had come to stand outside the open door—or maybe it was the dismayed glance Hally directed just past the girl's head that gave it away—Corinne turned to look right at him as she raged, "And I hate *him*."

Chapter Three

The expression of raw hurt on Mike Parker's face before he blanked it as deliberately as if he'd pulled down a shade, stayed with Hally as she slowly drove her car toward home. The spare tire did not allow for speed, which was just as well as she was in a meandering frame of mind after all the drama and trauma of the past several hours. She stopped briefly at the service station and dropped off her tire to be fixed.

Poor Mike, she thought. And poor Corinne, too. It would take a lot of time, patience and love for those two to find their way to each other. She ought to know; she and her father hadn't found that way yet. And it was what—ten years later? Something like that.

The only thing Mike and Cory had going for them that was different from Hally's situation with her father, was that Mike was *there*. His "defection" was not a fact, but a fixated notion that Corinne had come to wholly *embrace* as fact.

Doctor James McKenzie, on the other hand had, after years of philandering and sporadic, overstrict parenting, literally abandoned his wife and emotionally deserted his two daughters to marry his already-pregnant-with-his-child receptionist.

Hally pulled a face. Now thirty-four, Sweet Eva—their stepmother—was the same age as Hally's sister Morgan, and only two years older than Hally herself.

It had all been rather sordid and sad, and to this day relations between Hally and her father were strained and contact practically nonexistent. Hally had only seen her father's new wife and little half brother, now nine, a handful of times at a distance.

Stoutly in her mother's camp, it was Hally's choice to maintain the animosity, to ignore James McKenzie's occasional olive branches and overtures. Reestablishing a cordial relationship with her father would have made her feel disloyal to her mother. Her sister, Morgan, did not see things that way. Morgan had always been their father's pet, of course. And though she'd initially been hurt by his defection, with marriage and the birth of her own little boy— Kenny, now six—all had apparently been forgiven. Why, she even stayed in her father's house during her infrequent visits to Long Beach.

Well, to each his or her own, Hally thought, a little righteously. But, seeing again in her mind's eye Michael Parker's look of anguish at Corinne's hateful words, she wondered for the first time if her unrelenting attitude might not be causing her own father pain, as well.

Nonsense. Pulling into her drive, Hally resolutely brushed that unsettling notion aside. James McKenzie was much too arrogant and successful to let something as minor as the loss of one daughter's trust and affection wound him in any way. Especially with his other daughter as doting as ever.

Getting out of the car, Hally absently glanced at her mother's side of the house. No lights. She'd gone out.

Hally let herself into the house with a twinge of disappointment—some of her mother's tea and sympathy would have been a good antidote to everything that had gone before. She sighed and resigned herself to a hot shower and some tea on her own.

She was greeted in the kitchen by an indignant Chaucer. Crouching and scooping the loudly meowing cat up for a hug, Hally hurried to apologize. "Did you get trapped in the house, you silly old thing, you?"

Chaucer was not big on displays of affection, however, and soon squirmed to be free. "Well, off you go then," Hally groused good-naturedly as she let him out the back door. "Have fun...."

With a sigh—the house seemed strangely quiet and empty to her—she returned to the kitchen. She stood and looked around, irresolute. Was she hungry? She hadn't eaten and a while ago she'd been starving. But somehow food held no appeal now. A novel occurrence. Maybe losing that five pounds wouldn't be so difficult, after all.

Rolling her eyes, she considered a cup of hot tea but, spotting the blinking red light on the telephone console, dismissed that notion, too. Crossing over to the small planning desk, she pressed the Play button on the answering machine. Wine, she mused as the tape rewound with an audible whir. A nice glass of Chardonnay, that's what she wanted.

There were obviously several messages that always seemed to send her dinosaur of a machine into a tailspin. It took forever to rewind to the beginning of the tape. As she poured the wine Hally decided she'd simply have to get with the program and order voice mail.

"Hally!" *Ah, it speaks.*

Setting down her glass, Hally picked up a pencil and bent over the desk, poised to jot down names and phone numbers. This was Morgan, however, sounding distraught. Of course, she often did. "Do you know where Mother is tonight? I've been calling and calling. And what are you up to, anyway? Phone me.''

Right. Hally rolled her eyes. With Morgan, who now lived in Detroit, everything became a crisis when she thought she was being excluded from the loop of family news.

"Hey, why weren't you at aerobics?" Garnet Bloom- field. "I knew you'd chicken out, McKenzie. God will get you for that! I want to hear from you and it better be good. Signed, your conscience."

Oh, brother. Straightening, Hally tossed down the pen- cil. She massaged an ache in the small of her back. She was thinking nothing was going to be important enough to write down when the next message had her scrambling for the pencil and notepad.

"Ms. Mckenzie. This is Sergeant O'Rourke, L.B.P.D. Don't be alarmed, but please give me a call at 555-5000, extension 24. It's in regard to your mother. Thank you."

Oh, dear God. Hally sank down onto the chair in front of the desk and had to listen to the message twice more before she got the sergeant's telephone number down on paper. Her hand shook as she stabbed the digits and pressed the phone to her ear.

She gave the extension number when the police operator answered. It seemed to take forever before a male voice barked, "O'Rourke."

"Um." Nerves momentarily rendered Hally incoherent. She took a deep breath. "This is Hally McKenzie returning your call."

"Ah, yes," the officer said, his tone a bit less brisk. "Ms. McKenzie…"

"Has something happened to my mother?" Hally asked, bursting into the policeman's slight pause. He was no doubt finding his notes on the case or some such, part of her brain thought irrelevantly.

"She's all right," Sergeant O'Rourke assured her. "But

she asked me to give you a call and to say would you pack an overnight bag and bring it to Memorial Hospital, room number—''

"Hospital!" Hally heard nothing beyond that dreaded word. She surged up off the chair. "What's wrong with her? What happened? Why wasn't I—"

"She says she tried to call you. You didn't answer."

The phone call.

"She hung up before I could get the phone," Hally explained tonelessly. Was there to be no end to disaster tonight? "She didn't leave a message."

"Yeah, well. She was in pretty bad shape, just barely managed to dial 9-1-1. She fell into some glass. Lacerations…''

"Oh—" With an inarticulate sound of distress, Hally pressed a hand against her mouth. *Not her hands!* She swallowed down nausea at the visions the officer's words conjured up. "What was that room number again?"

The pencil jerked in her hand as she wrote down what the sergeant said.

Operating in a daze, she went over to her mother's side of the house and stuffed toiletries, undergarments and anything else that seemed necessary into a bag. And all the while she thanked the Lord that her mother's studio was out in the garage, meaning she wouldn't have to look at the accident's bloody evidence. She had never been able to stomach the sight of blood. This queasiness was one of the many things her father—a surgeon—had endlessly criticized her for.

On the way to the hospital Hally wondered if she should have called Morgan to apprise her of the situation, but then decided she'd do so after she'd seen their mother and taken stock of the situation firsthand. The last thing she needed after everything else that had occurred today, was to listen to her highly pregnant-with-her-second-child and therefore even-more-easily-unhinged older sister.

Bumping into James McKenzie at the door of her mother's room was another thing Hally could have lived without.

"Father," she exclaimed, too tired and rattled to try to keep the appalled tone out of her voice or to edit her words for diplomacy. "What in the world are you doing here?"

"Well, I *am* a doctor," her father said mildly, looking Hally up and down in that way he had, that way that had always made her feel inadequate. It galled her to realize it still did. "And this *is* my hospital," he went on. "At least to the extent that I'm the chief here."

"Oh. I didn't, er, didn't know…"

"There's a lot you don't know, Halloran."

"Yes, well…" Despising herself for reverting to the very behavior—awkward ineptness—that had always drawn scathing comments from her father, Hally clenched her teeth and met his gaze with much of the same youthful defiance that had always been her defense. And here she'd been so sure she had outgrown that sort of response, too. "If you'll let me by, I—I came to see my mother."

"Of course." James McKenzie stepped aside. "It seems your mother fell and hit her head on the edge of her workbench. There was some bleeding, but nothing too serious. She's sedated, but she'll be all right."

Hally drew herself in so that she could move past without touching him in any way. Her gaze flicked to his once more, and what she saw in his eyes made her gasp. He actually looked hurt.

Furious with herself even more than with her father, she jerked her eyes away and stumbled almost blindly into her mother's room.

The nurse at the bedside looked up at Hally's entrance. She put a finger to her lips. "She's just drifting off," she whispered in very British English as Hally tiptoed closer. "Doctor gave her a sedative."

Hally mutely nodded her understanding. She was still

undone by the unexpected emotions she'd glimpsed in her father's eyes, and horrified by the sight of her mother's bandaged right hand on top of the bedsheet. She let the bag drop to the floor and leaned closer to peer into the dear but pale and too-still features. They were usually so animated. A rather nasty-looking purple bump and bruise marred the high forehead.

Ever so gently, lovingly, Hally touched the injury, letting her finger trail down the velvety cheek before pulling her hand away. *I love you, Mom.*

"Concussion?" she asked in a low tone.

The nurse shook her head. "Doctor wouldn't have sedated her if he thought that. You're family, of course." It was a statement rather than a question.

Hally nodded. "Her daughter."

"Oh," the nurse said, her interest obviously aroused. "In that case, you're..."

"Doctor McKenzie's daughter, too," Hally finished for her. "Yes." Wanting to forestall any further comments, she asked, "Will my mother be asleep all night?"

"I would think so, yes."

"I've brought her some things." Hally picked up the bag. "Where should I put them?"

"In the nightstand would be fine," the nurse said, leaving the room. "She'll be discharged in the morning."

Hally took her time unpacking the small bag. Rather than hang it up, she draped her mother's robe over the foot of the bed. Likewise, she arranged the satin slippers she had packed so that they were ready to be stepped into should her mother need to get up in the night.

She glanced often at the still form on the bed, hoping against hope that her mother would wake and know she was there. When everything was done, feeling helpless, needing to be needed but realizing that there wasn't anything else she could do, Hally softly kissed her mother on the lips and took her reluctant leave.

"I'll be back, Mom," she whispered. "First thing in the morning."

After a drive home that was filled with a heavy silence neither Michael nor Corinne Parker was inclined to break, father and daughter walked single file into their house. Corinne would have proceeded straight to her room, but Mike stopped her.

"I want to talk to you." He jerked a chair away from the kitchen table and pointed to it. "Sit."

Folding her arms across her chest, ignoring the chair, Corinne pointedly propped her hip against the counter and didn't move.

A rage that was the culmination of everything that had gone before brought Mike over to her in one long stride. He gripped her upper arm with viselike strength.

"I said sit," he bellowed, yanking the chair closer still and pushing her down onto it. "And by damn you'll sit, young lady."

Releasing her as abruptly as he had grabbed her, Mike pivoted and stalked over to the window. He was breathing heavily as the veil of red fury slowly receded from in front of his eyes. Never could he remember having been this angry. He shoved a trembling hand through his hair, inhaling deeply and struggling for a modicum of calm before facing his daughter again.

"Things are going to change around here," he finally said when he trusted himself to be rational. "You are going to act like a civilized human being..."

"Yeah," Corinne drawled, her voice and expression full of contempt. "Like you just did, right?"

"Oh, no, you don't." Mike glared at her. "You're not going to turn the tables and lay a guilt trip on me for manhandling you just now. Granted, I lost my temper, but you'd push even a saint to mayhem with your stubbornness and rotten attitude. And it's going to stop."

"Pfuh." Lips twisted, her arms once again folded across her chest, Corinne turned her face aside as if bored.

Mike had to silently count to ten to keep himself from exploding all over again. He knew that if he hoped to get anywhere with her, it wouldn't be by shouting. On the other hand, he had no intention of letting her off the hook. She had become a liar, a thief and a truant. He intended to put a stop to those practices before they became ingrained.

He walked to the shelf, took down the porcelain cat and brought it over to her. He set it on the table. When she refused to look at it, he firmly but not roughly took her chin and forced her face around.

"There was two hundred dollars in that jar," he said. "Now there's seventy. I want to know what happened to the rest of it."

"How should I know?" Corinne muttered. But she wouldn't look at him, and her face flushed a deep red. The sight of it filled Mike with relief. It proved to him that she still had a conscience, that she wasn't too far gone to be reached.

"Look at me," he ordered, still holding her chin.

She complied with deliberate slowness, defiance blazing from her eyes.

He put his own face right in front of hers. "Where'd you get the money for the concert?"

She compressed her lips and said nothing.

"And for these rags you're wearing?" Mike pushed on, staring into eyes hot with resentment. "And for this?" He flicked a disgusted glance at the bleached mess of her hair. "Where did you get the money, Corinne?"

"What's the difference?" she surprised him by suddenly, heatedly exclaiming. He had been braced for more silence. "You don't care!"

Wrenching out of his light hold, she jumped to her feet and faced him with both hands balled into fists. "I'm surprised you even noticed, you're so busy nagging at me all the time to clean up my room and do dishes and take out the trash. That's all I am to you—aren't I?—a maid. You don't care what I do, where I go, how I feel. You never ask me how I like it here, what I think about school or anything. You hate me!''

"I do not!" Mike said vehemently. "My God, Cory, I love you! You're my child, you're all I've got!"

But she wasn't listening, just kept on ranting. "And I hate it here. I hate this stupid town, I hate this crummy house, and I hate living with you. I want to go home! Why can't you just let me go ho-oome…''

The last was a wail of such anguish, Mike felt as if his heart was being torn from his chest. Near tears himself, he caught Corinne by the shoulder when, wildly sobbing, she would have rushed from the room. He detained her struggling form with gentle force. Turning her toward him, he wrapped his arms around her and crooned soothingly as she wept against his chest. Holding her, he was struck by the frailty of her adolescent body, a frailty that wasn't ordinarily apparent, hidden beneath layers of baggy, oversize clothes and further disguised by her attitude of snotty standoffishness.

"Cory, baby," he murmured, stroking her back, rocking her gently from side to side. "Don't cry so. Please, don't cry. We'll work it out…''

"I don't want to work it out!" Cory tore out of his embrace. Stamping her foot, she raised a face that was wet with tears, streaked with the colors of the rainbow from her makeup and distorted into an ugly mask. "I don't want to be here. I don't want to be with you. And you can't make me.''

Stunned, this time Mike didn't try to stop her headlong flight from the room. He stood unmoving, only flinching slightly at the slam of her door.

He, who had fought the elements on nearly every continent, who had supervised scores of some of the roughest men on the globe, who had faced and stood against rebels and guerrillas, sheiks and corporate heads, had been utterly and totally defeated by the poisoned tongue of his fourteen-year-old daughter.

Tomorrow he would begin making arrangements to send her back home.

Hally didn't make it to school in time for her appointment with Mike and Corinne Parker. Nor, in the interest of reclaiming some of the professional detachment she found it so difficult to maintain with this particular student and parent, did she try to contact them at their home. Instead she called the principal's office first thing in the morning to arrange for a sub to take her morning English classes, as well as to request that Gilbert Smith meet with Mike and make her apologies. She also asked that Gil tell Mike she would catch Corinne after lunch and have a talk with her then.

She was on her way to the school now, after a morning almost as full of surprises as the previous night had been, though a good deal less traumatic.

She had arrived at the hospital just after seven, still groggy from a restless night of tossing and turning, and jumbled dreams that featured Mike Parker and her father in interchangeable roles. Freud would probably have had a field day with that.

She'd been shocked to see a uniformed policeman at her mother's bedside. And it was no doubt testimony to her rattled state of nerves that the first thought popping into her head had been, Good grief, someone tried to kill her. This was accompanied by visions of her father bent on mayhem.

Which—horrendous though the thought had been—wasn't quite as farfetched and wild a notion as it might have been. Both extremely volatile individuals, her parents had had some pretty violent set-tos prior to their divorce.

But, of course, nothing like murder had occurred. Or violence of any sort, for that matter. Her mother was hale and hearty outside of the injuries from her fall, and as giddy as a young girl with her unhurt hand nestled in Police Sergeant William O'Rourke's ruddy paw.

She'd hastily withdrawn it when Hally had stepped up to the bed. "Hally, darling," she'd exclaimed, and much to Hally's consternation actually blushed. "Bill... I mean, Sergeant O'Rourke was kind enough to stop by to see how I was."

At seven in the morning? Keeping that thought to herself, Hally had nodded and smiled as if it were perfectly natural to come upon her mother entertaining male visitors at her bedside at the crack of dawn.

"We spoke on the phone," she'd said to the sergeant.

"Right." He'd edged away, a big, brawny man with an honest face and freckles, and an adoring expression in his eyes when he looked at her mother.

"I'll call you later then, Edith," he'd said from the door. And to Hally, "Nice meeting you."

"And you," Hally had murmured. When the door closed behind him, she turned to her mother, eyebrows raised. "Care to tell me what's going on, Mother dear?"

Recalling the moment, Hally pulled into her reserved spot in the school parking lot with a chuckle and an amazed shake of the head. It seemed the good sergeant had made her mother's acquaintance several weeks ago in the line of duty—he had issued her a speeding ticket. He had apparently been instantly smitten, and so rattled by that discovery that he'd failed to return to Edith her driver's license.

So he had later stopped by the house with it, and—as Hally's mother had put it—one thing had led to another.

And a good thing, too, she had told Hally emphatically,

because if Bill hadn't made one of his impromptu visits to her studio yesterday afternoon, heaven only knew what might have become of her. The bump on the head had rendered her momentarily unconscious, and she had used the speed dial digit to call Hally upon coming to.

But then she'd swooned again at the sight of all that blood. "You know I'm as bad as you when it comes to blood, Hally, dear." Which was when Bill had walked in.

"It was serendipity, darling," Edith proclaimed, and her very drama as much as anything else convinced Hally that her mother was on the mend. "Our karmas are joined, Bill's and mine...."

"More power to you, Mother," Hally muttered, and admitted to being a little envious as she hurried up the steps to the school's huge double doors. There were times when she, too, wouldn't mind if some nice man's karma were to meet up with hers.

For some reason that brought Michael Parker back to mind, and he stayed there as she hurried to the teachers' lounge. Not because he was attractive in his not-really-handsome way and a widower, which of course he was, but because she felt a little guilty about having stood him up that morning.

And because the situation with his daughter touched her. There, she'd admitted it. He seemed to take it all so very much to heart. He was so genuinely bewildered, hurt and at a loss, and he blamed himself far more than he probably should.

As a woman, it was clear to Hally that that little vixen of a daughter of his played on that guilt for all she was worth.

The man needed an ally. But who? Hally sighed, squelching the impulse to volunteer herself for the job. As if she didn't have enough on her plate, what with her mother, Gil, and all those preparations for her Italian sabbatical. She would work with the girl here at school, but other than that....

"B.J., hi." Hally walked into the teachers' lounge to find Birgit James, the sub who had taken her classes that morning, just finishing her lunch. "I was hoping you'd still be around. Thanks for filling in at such short notice."

"You'd do the same for me," Birgit averred. "How's your mother?"

"Doing great, thank you." Hally hung up her denim jacket. "Any problems?"

Birgit laughed. "Nothing I couldn't handle."

"Jackie Sims," Hally stated dryly. She checked her face in her compact mirror. Controlling the urge to mess with the pimple on her chin, she grimaced and snapped it shut. "Mischief is that boy's middle name. How was the Parker girl? Corinne?"

"Parker. Uh-oh." Birgit slapped the side of her head with the flat of her hand. "I would've forgotten—he was looking for you. Mr. Parker."

"He was?" Hally frowned. "I had asked that Gil talk to him and explain."

"Gil's got the flu or something," another teacher, a colleague of Gilbert Smith's from the math department, put in. "He didn't come in today."

"Oh, great." Hally mentally flung up her hands. Was there a conspiracy afoot to complicate her life?

"Was he upset?" she asked, wondering what Mike must think of her for not being there as agreed. "And was the girl all right?" She pressed on without giving Birgit a chance to answer the first question. "His daughter, I mean?"

"Well..." B.J. wrinkled her forehead. "I seem to remember she asked to go to the rest room about halfway through the hour. But you know, now that you mention it, I don't recall her coming back to class...."

"Oh, swell." Hally closed her eyes in despair. "She's done it again."

All right, young lady, Hally thought grimly a few minutes later as she stalked out of the teachers' lounge after getting Birgit to handle her afternoon sessions, too. Fun and games are over.

Detouring past her office, she telephoned Mike Parker at his place of work to request an immediate meeting. Only to be informed by the female voice on the other end that Mr. Parker had taken a couple of days personal leave and would not be in the rest of the week.

Wonderful. Dropping the phone on its cradle, Hally glared at the outdated instrument, deep in thought. She had two choices—phone Michael Parker at home or go look him up in person.

Every instinct told her to call and let it go at that. "Your daughter once again skipped school, Mr. Parker. Handle it."

Yeah, right. Hally sighed. Like it or not, she was involved in this. And maybe if she'd been there this morning...

"All right, all right," she muttered crossly. *Mea culpa.* "I'm going."

Still muttering, she jotted down the Parker address and home phone. Moments later, she was on her way.

She had no trouble finding the place. It was in a once posh, now slightly seedy neighborhood a few blocks from the beach. Many of the former mansions had been converted into rooming houses, or chopped up into apartments.

The Parker house was a small bungalow the siding of which had been painted a rather unfortunate—in Hally's opinion—pink. Gazing at it with a shudder as she parked her car at the curb and got out, she caught herself hoping

Mike was only renting. Only to immediately remind herself that it didn't matter to her one way or the other.

His Buick was parked at the curb two cars ahead of hers. Which meant he was home. With luck, his daughter was, too, and they could settle this business once and for all. She had her Italian language class to go to tonight.

Squaring her shoulders, and doing her best to ignore the butterflies that had unaccountably taken wing in her stomach, she strode up the uneven cement walk, up three cracked concrete steps, and knocked on the front door.

She frowned as from inside a female voice trilled, ''Just a minute.''

Corinne? No way. Too cheerful. Too smoky-rough.

The door opened and Hally's eyes widened as they settled on the same redhead who had soaked Mike Parker's shirtfront at the stadium the night before. Bruises were visible on her bare arms, but her face looked much improved. Or maybe that inch of makeup she wore just made it seem so.

In any case, Hally hardly noticed since her eyes were riveted on the woman's curvaceous body sheathed in a diaphanous negligee that drew attention to, rather than covered, the micro bikini she had on underneath.

Chapter Four

"**W**ell, hi, hon," the woman purred, and with such a disarming lack of self-consciousness that Hally couldn't help but be impressed even as an unpleasant burning sensation permeated her midsection. But while she was loathe to speculate on its cause, she did wonder what this woman was to Michael Parker.

"Hello." She couldn't keep the note of chilly reserve from her voice. She would have used that tone on anyone *un*dressed like that in the middle of the day. "Is, er, Mr. Parker available?"

"Well, now, that all depends," the other woman purred throatily in a pointed double entendre that Hally decided it would be best to ignore.

"I'm Corinne's teacher," she said repressively.

Just then the man she was here to see moved into view. One glance showed him to be completely dressed in jeans and a polo shirt. Some of the tension in Hally's stomach eased. He even wore shoes. Not to mention a decidedly harried expression that was a far cry from the look of someone recently tumbled and physically sated.

"Hal—Ms. McKenzie!" There was surprise but no guilt in his tone.

And as his eyes slid from her to the scantily clad other woman, it was almost comical to see the parade of expressions that marched across his rugged face. Surprise gave way to shock, to red-faced chagrin and, finally, to patent exasperation.

"For crying out loud, Pamela, what're you doing here in that getup?"

Which was certainly something Hally wanted to know.

Pamela seemed unperturbed. She shrugged negligently, causing the open peignoir to provocatively slide off one shoulder.

Hally, herself too insecure about her body to even wear a bikini at the beach, found herself envying the woman's aplomb.

"I came to show you my bruises," the redhead told Mike with a pout that Hally considered pretty ridiculous for such a mature woman. "Since you were on the phone, I simply took off my coat and turned on my favorite soap while I waited for you to get done."

"Look, if this is a bad time…?" Hally interrupted, a bit testily in view of the irritating byplay she was forced to witness between Mike Parker and this…this… She couldn't think of a fitting appellation but was pretty sure it would not have been nice.

Mike hastened to assure Hally that this was a perfectly good time for whatever it was she needed to see him about. "Pam was just leaving," he said, retrieving the redhead's raincoat from the sofa and handing it to her. "Weren't you, Pamela?"

Pamela tossed her head like a spirited mare, looked Hally up and down with one long sweep of her artificial lashes and, dangling the light coat from one finger, sashayed out the front door.

Standing aside to let her pass, Hally was momentarily

bathed in a cloud of cloying perfume. It caused her to sneeze three times in rapid succession.

"Catching something?" Mike Parker asked, inviting Hally to enter with a sweep of his hand.

She gave him an arch look. "Seems to me your lady friend stands a better chance of catching something than I do."

"She's not my lady friend." Mike closed the door, indicating with another gesture that Hally should be seated. "Only a neighbor."

After a quick glance around the room—expensive furniture arranged in utilitarian fashion, no knickknacks, no warmth—Hally perched on the sofa. She primly tucked down her short skirt and fleetingly tried to recall when she'd last shaved her legs. "Chummy neighbor."

"Yes, well..." Mike lowered himself onto the upholstered arm of the deep easy chair across from her. With what Hally considered a most disconcerting flash of humor he said, "I figured this being Southern California, Pam was the norm."

Hally flashed him a glance of mock outrage. "Being Southern California born and raised, I resent such generalizations and assure you she isn't."

"I stand corrected," Mike said with a grin that took years off his face.

Though it was gone almost before it had fully formed, Hally's heart skipped a beat in response to it. She quickly looked down at her hands. "I'm sorry I wasn't at school this morning," she said.

"I'm sure you didn't come here in the middle of the day just to tell me that."

"No, of course not." She raised her head and, meeting his gaze, found it once again somber and dark. His strong features, too, were lined by immeasurable weariness and sorrow. She hated to add to his troubles but had no choice, of course. "The reason I came is that Corinne skipped out on us again. She's not at school."

"Not at school?" Mike repeated, his upper body snapping forward as though he'd been socked in the back. His tone was disbelieving. "Why that's impossible. I walked her right to the classroom door."

"I know." Hally moved her shoulder in a helpless, commiserating half shrug. "I'm told she asked to go to the washroom and didn't return. It's an easy enough trick to pull for a girl of Corinne's determination."

"Maybe if you'd been there this morning to talk to her, as you said, she wouldn't now be missing," Mike Parker admonished unexpectedly.

Affronted, Hally pulled herself sharply erect. Although she had already similarly blamed herself, she didn't appreciate the charge coming from him. She did have a life of her own, after all.

"Something unavoidable and personal came up," she said stiffly, seeking refuge in the kind of detached professionalism she should be, but was unfortunately far from, feeling. "And the teacher who was supposed to have conveyed that to you apparently called in sick with the flu."

"Unavoidable and personal," Mike repeated with an ironic twist to his mouth. "My daughter's and my problems certainly don't fit either of those categories. We're strictly in the line of duty..."

"If that were so, I would hardly be here," Hally responded defensively, even as she told herself she did not owe this man any explanations. "For your information, I had to pick my mother up from the hospital and get her settled at home."

"I'm sorry." Mike shook his head with immediate contrition. He blew out a sigh. "I don't know what's the matter with me. I'm not usually a whiner. All I can say in my defense is—it's been a helluva twenty-four hours."

Instantly disarmed by this rueful declaration, Hally slumped. "It's been pretty hairy for me, too."

"I know." They looked at each other, both aware of, and startled by, some undefinable something passing between them as the moment lengthened.

Unable to look away, Hally felt her heart beating high in her throat, which had gone as dry as the Mojave Desert. A long silence hummed between them.

And then Mike abruptly stood. He cleared his throat. "I, uh, appreciate everything you've done." His tone was gruff. "Thanks for coming by."

Shaky in the aftermath of the quivering excitement their prolonged eye contact had unleashed, and taken aback by what was clearly a dismissal, Hally hastily rose in response to it. *All right,* she inwardly sniffed, *if that's the way you want it, I'm out of here.*

Reaching for her shoulder bag, however, she happened to glance at his ashen face and relented. "Any ideas where your daughter might be?"

Mike shook his head. "No."

"Then how will you find her?"

"I don't know."

"I came here to offer my help, Mr. Parker," Hally said a little stiffly.

Mike's expression remained unreadable. "And like I said, I appreciate it." He opened the door and stood beside it, pointedly waiting for Hally to leave.

She didn't. She stopped in front of him. "What are you planning to do after you find her?"

He hesitated, then curtly said, "I'm sending her back to Idaho."

"What?"

Mike shrugged off Hally's startled disbelief. His expression matched the grim resolve in his tone. "I had more or less made up my mind to do that anyway, after last

night. She and I had a talk after we got back here that
didn't go well.

"And that's putting it mildly," he added with a humorless little laugh. "She's been stealing money from me
and apparently couldn't care less."

"Oh, I'm sure that she does care," Hally immediately
declared. A toucher, she had to consciously restrain herself
from putting a hand on Mike Parker's arm in a gesture of
empathy and support. Somehow she sensed that he was
trying very hard to keep her at a distance, just as she was
trying to do with him. She didn't care to dwell on the
implications of that.

"She's rebelling," she said rather lamely.

"No kidding." Mike's tone was dry. And the look that
accompanied it reminded Hally that he didn't have much
patience with platitudes. She felt ashamed for having offered one.

While she still fumbled for something conciliatory to
say, Mike briskly said, "In any case, I called my wife's
folks to set things up."

"Then it's already settled?" Hally asked with incredu-
lity and a sense of disappointment that startled her. She
ought to be glad to have this situation off her hands.

"Unfortunately not quite," Mike said, and Hally relaxed
a little. "They're going on a cruise for a month."

"Well, then, why not use that time to—"

"No." Apparently Mike knew what she'd been going
to say. "I'm not putting up with her shenanigans for one
more day, let alone a month. The Lord only knows the
kind of irreparable trouble she'd get herself into in that
period of time. Getting her away from here is the only
way."

"It really isn't, you know," Hally said. She strongly
suspected that Mike's decision was an act of desperation,
one he hated being driven to. "There is another way, if
you'd be willing to work with me."

"Work with you to do what?" Mike demanded, not very graciously.

But he did close the front door again, something Hally took as a sign of encouragement.

"To turn her around," she said, and stayed on his heels when Mike abruptly headed for the kitchen.

She watched him fill a glass of water from the tap, and shook her head no when he offered it to her before draining it himself.

"Deep down she really wants to, you know," Hally said, struggling not to become sidetracked by the fascinating sight of Michael Parker's Adam's apple moving up and down as he drank. "Be turned around by you, I mean."

Swiping the back of his hand across his mouth, Mike set down the glass. His eyes fixing on something outside, he stared through the curtainless window and gave a mirthless little chuckle. "If she does, she's got a helluva way of showing it."

"I know." Because her hands itched to reach out and touch him, Hally forced her eyes away from his strong, troubled profile. She glanced around the kitchen. It was a mess. Being a neatnick, as well as glad to have found something acceptable to do with her hands, she began gathering up dirty dishes. She stacked them in the sink. "The feelings daughters have for their fathers are complicated at best."

"So I've found out." Scowling, Mike took the box of cereal Hally had taken off the table and stashed it in the cupboard.

Hally handed him the sugar bowl, saying, "What we need to figure out is *why* she is so terribly angry with you. Because that's really what all this *hate* talk is about, you know—*anger*. Corinne is angry with herself because she loves and needs you in spite of the fact that, in her mind, you have let her down. This, in turn, makes her angry with you. So the thing to find out is—how have you let her down? In her perception.''

"Psychology 101?" Mike's forceful slam of the cupboard door loudly communicated his disdain.

Hally only managed to choke back an affronted retort by reminding herself that being in pain and feeling vulnerable was what put him on the defensive.

"To tell you the truth, it's more personal than that," she said. "My father and I have been...at odds, shall we say, for some time."

"And still are?"

"Well...yes." Avoiding Mike's challenging stare, Hally concentrated on drying her hands on the wilted tea towel that had graced the back of a chair. She braced herself for what Mike would surely have to say.

He said it immediately. And scathingly. "You can't fix your own problems, but you want to tell me—"

"I want to *tell* you nothing." Hally heatedly cut him off. "What I'm willing to *do* is to *help* get your daughter off this self-destructive course she's embarked on. That's all. Working out the emotional stuff is strictly up to you and her. Just as it's up to my father and me to work out ours."

"Have you tried?" Mike asked quietly.

Caught off guard, Hally bit her lip with a negative jerk of the head. To avoid letting him see that this pained her, she opened the dishwasher and loaded the dishes she had stacked in the sink.

"Has *he*?"

Resenting being questioned, Hally's curt nod was her way of conceding tit for tat. She was butting into Mike Parker's personal affairs and that, she supposed, gave him the right to poke into hers. Within limits.

Which he reached when he murmured, "So it's do as I say, not do as I do, is that it?"

"Yes." Hally closed the dishwasher door with a decisive click and swung around. "Why is Corinne angry with you?"

Mike frowned at Hally's bristling stance, as well as at his own incomprehensible desire to ask her more questions about herself. His sole concern ought to be his daughter, his *missing* daughter, for crying out loud.

"You're asking a lot of questions," he said testily. "But you don't give a lot of answers."

"True." Hally didn't flinch. "But then, I'm not the one in trouble here."

"Aren't you?"

"No," Hally said with finality. "At least not to the extent that it's your business."

"I see." In the weighty silence that followed, their gazes dueled. Neither, it seemed, was willing to cave in first.

At length Hally drew a breath and repeated her question. "Why do you think your daughter's angry with you, Mr. Parker?"

"All right." With a sigh, Mike capitulated. Like it or not, he did need help and this woman was offering it. In turn it behooved him not to antagonize her. He said, "My overseas job, for one thing. I was never there for those little milestones kids consider so important. And then there's the fact that I didn't come home when her mother took sick and died."

He tried to sound nonchalant, but couldn't quite hide the fact that Cory's charges were eating him up inside and making him wonder if dreams of a horse ranch really should have been more important than a father's obligation to his only child.

And about Rebecca. Was it because of her wishes and because of the way she had changed, or because of *his* own cowardice that he'd stayed on the job during her illness?

"Right now we need the money you earn more than we

need you to be home," she had told him in that terrible phone conversation that turned out to be the last time he would ever hear her voice. "And anyway, I'm vain enough to want you to remember me the way I was, not the way I am now..."

"What about Cory?" he had asked.

"My folks're with her. She's fine...."

But Cory hadn't been fine. She had been furious with him, had raged at him and called him awful names because he hadn't come home until the funeral.

"Michael?" Halloran McKenzie's light touch on the arm snapped Mike out of his dark reverie.

"Cory never forgave me for that," he said heavily. "Nor for going away again afterward. If only—"

An expression of anguish distorted his face and he quickly averted it. His voice shook. "If only I could be sure that I can reach her and turn her around..."

"There are no guarantees," honesty prompted Hally to admit. "But surely trying is better than doing nothing at all, which in my opinion sending her back to Idaho would amount to. Sending her back is tantamount to giving up and giving in to her. And giving in to her is the easy way out."

Though Hally spoke softly, there was steel in her tone. "Indulgence is the last thing your daughter needs from you right now. What she does need is for you to hang tough. She needs to know that you're not skipping out when the going gets rough. That you'll be there for her, no matter what. She loves you, Michael, in spite of what she says. But she doesn't dare trust you, doesn't dare let herself believe that you will stick around. By being as nasty and obnoxious as possible, she is testing you to see if you'll turn your back on her.

"Which is what you will be doing if you ship her back to Idaho. You might think you're giving her what she wants, but what you're really doing is failing her test."

Mike took his time digesting all that. He recognized Hally's words as truth, but wasn't sure he could deal with that truth or fulfill the expectations that truth implied.

But he also knew he'd never forgive himself if he knowingly failed his child.

There's nothing easy about raising a kid. Who had said that? Mike couldn't remember the person, but he did recall the rest of what had been said. *And that is what makes it worthwhile.*

"So where do I go from here?" he asked.

"We find Corinne."

"We?"

"Yes. We." Even as she said it, Hally was calling herself seven kinds of a fool. *You don't have time for this. You're supposed to have priorities.*

Well, her priorities had just been shuffled around a bit. "I'll help if you want."

"I want," Mike conceded heavily. He was way out of his depth and sinking deeper all the time. He'd be a fool not to take the hand this woman offered. He rubbed his face. "So what do we do?"

"Well." Hally took a deep breath. "If you'll recall, the police released your daughter into your custody last night. In a way, that's like letting her out on bail. Corinne skipped bail…"

Mike stared at her, grappling with what she was implying. "You're saying have the police pick her up?"

"Well?" Hally's expression was challenging. "We're talking a dose of tough love here, Mr. Parker. Have they set a hearing date?"

"Yeah. Day after tomorrow, ten in the morning."

"Maybe it would teach her a lesson if she were kept in jail overnight."

"In jail?" Mike gaped at Hally as if she had lost her mind. "What in hell would that teach her?"

"That actions have consequences."

"And how docs that demonstrate that I'm there for her?"

"It doesn't. But your being by her side at the hearing, standing up for her and showing you believe in her innocence, will. Also, your going into the police station with me tomorrow and arranging—as far as she is concerned with great difficulty—for her to be released into my custody for that second night would, I'm sure, make her see that you're in her corner.

"Michael," Hally said persuasively when he still hesitated. "Only something drastic will shock Corinne into realizing that the direction she's headed is not the smart way to go."

"I know." Staring out the window and into space once again, Mike blew out a long, shaky breath. He wished Rebecca were here to tell him what was best. But she wasn't.

This woman, on the other hand, this Halloran Mc-Kenzie, was. What's more, she was willing to help; she was on his side.

After a month of struggling along on his own, having an ally felt too good to give up.

"All right." He pushed away from the counter and jerked his head in a decisive nod. "Let's do it."

After explaining to Mike how she planned to proceed, Hally took care of the preliminaries in the course of one long phone conversation with her mother's latest admirer—Sergeant William O'Rourke. He took it from there.

Within two hours Corinne had been nabbed at a large discount store across town where she had had the bad sense to shoplift a cheap tube of lipstick. As was customary, after confronting Corinne, store security had called in the police and they, in turn, took the girl into custody.

O'Rourke was notified, whereupon he called Hally, who

had left Mike to go to the duplex and look in on her mother.

"I'll meet you at the station," Hally hastily told Mike in a phone call from Edith's just before bolting out the door.

An odd sense of déjà vu befell her as she pulled up at the curb in just about the same spot her yellow Bug had occupied the previous night. She scowled at the newly repaired front tire as she got out of the car and silently forbade it to do something cute like go flat on her once again. Hurrying up the sidewalk, she passed Mike's car, which was parked a little closer to the precinct house this time.

The air inside the station was as stale as it had been last night, too, though less oppressive because there weren't nearly as many people crowding the room.

Mike leaped to his feet the moment he spotted her pushing through the front door. "What took you so long?"

Realizing it was stress that made him so impatient, Hally just mutely grabbed his hand and gave it a reassuring squeeze. She ended the contact almost immediately; the heat of his skin against the coolness of hers had unleashed a most disturbing flutter in her stomach.

"Sergeant O'Rourke, please," she said to the duty officer at the counter. "It's Hally McKenzie and Michael Parker."

The officer spoke into a dingy black phone. Dropping it back on its cradle, he curtly said, "Third door on the left."

Their chat with the sergeant was brief. Corinne had been given the right to make a phone call, which she had refused. She was being sullen and uncommunicative. Having now experienced her truculence firsthand, O'Rourke declared himself somewhat more amenable to Hally's suggestion that keeping the girl incarcerated overnight would teach her a valuable lesson.

"The coupl'a cells we have out back aren't exactly Sing-Sing," he said gruffly, "but, hell, they're a far cry from what she's probably used to. Mind you, we wouldn't ordinarily keep a little gal like her with no priors locked up. Parents and their attorneys would have our hides. But…''

Still looking troubled, he spread his hands. Mike spoke up; so far Hally, in her capacity as Corinne's teacher and counselor had done all the talking.

''Could I—we—see her a minute?''

''Don't see why not.'' It was clear by the almost eager way the sergeant left his office that he hoped a face-to-face meeting would change Mike's and Hally's minds about leaving the girl in jail.

''That man's not nearly as tough as he looks,'' Mike remarked with a frowning glare at O'Rourke's wide, re-treating back.

Hally chuckled, recalling the big man's teddy-bear sweetness at her mother's bedside. ''Lucky for us, I would say.''

She followed suit when Mike scrambled to his feet as Corinne was ushered into O'Rourke's crowded office, which, with her added presence, seemed frighteningly claustrophobic.

Eyes drawn as if by magnets to the handcuffs around his daughter's bony little wrists, Mike flinched as though he'd been struck. Outrage and pain speared through him like the cut of a knife and his gaze flew to the sergeant's. ''What in the hell are you doing, handcuffing my daughter like some common criminal?''

''Regulations, sir,'' O'Rourke said formally. But his eyes questioned Mike's willingness to see this thing through.

And suddenly Mike no longer wanted to. What had he been thinking? He was unable to tear his gaze away from the wraithlike form dressed in oversize hand-me-downs. Dear God, this was his child. And those were Becky's eyes, for all they were outrageously outlined in black and dully staring back at him out of a chalk white face.

"Cory...." He took a step toward her, hand outstretched.

Corinne shrank away from him. Her eyes came alive, and she glared at him as though he were some monster about to strike. She turned to the sergeant, presenting Mike and Hally with her back. "I wanna go back to my cell."

It was Hally who nodded in response to O'Rourke's quick, questioning glance. Mike was too stricken, too stunned by this latest rejection to be able to say anything at all. He stood stock-still, his hand still outstretched.

Watching him with helpless empathy, Hally dug her nails into the palms of her own tightly curled hands. She wanted to go to him, somehow comfort him, but tension emanated from Mike like radiation from a faulty reactor and she just didn't dare approach him.

"Mike," she finally said, very softly.

But he started as if she had shouted his name. His hand dropped to his side. Slowly he turned toward her. He stared at her as if at a complete stranger. "This isn't going to work," he said tonelessly.

"Yes, it is." No longer hesitant, Hally took his arm and shook it as if to wake him up. "I never said it was going to be easy."

"No, you didn't. But this—" his aimless gesture encompassed the drab little office "—this is all so much worse than I thought it would be."

"It's just for one night." Still holding his arm, Hally forced Mike to look at her, willing him to regain his earlier resolve.

Their eyes locked as Mike returned her urgent gaze with brooding intensity. After a long, tense moment, he bowed his head and his shoulders slumped. "Oh, God," he said raggedly, making Hally wonder if he was addressing her

or the mighty creator Himself. "I sure hope you know
what you're doing."

They were both running on empty by the time they ex-
ited the police station. They stood by Mike's car, irresolute, feeling strangely let down and at loose ends. They
should say goodbye and each go their own way. They were
strangers, linked only by a common interest in a very confused and bereaved young girl.

Or so they tried to tell themselves.

"Well." Hally looked down at her toe, nudging an in-
trepid weed growing out of the crack in the sidewalk. "I
guess this is it for today."

"Yeah, I guess." Mike fingered his keys, lips pursed,
frowning. His head hurt. He was hungry. And he dreaded
more than anything the thought of going home alone to
the house he shared with Corinne. "I, uh…"

He just barely stopped himself from asking what he
knew would probably be just one more imposition for this
woman who had already given so much of her time to his
and his daughter's troubles. She probably had plans for
dinner. After all, she had lived here all her life. She had
friends here. Family…

"I guess I'll see you."

"Absolutely," Hally said, much more heartily than
Mike's unenthusiastic remark merited. "I'll call you tomorrow, just as soon as I get Corinne settled at my house."

She peered up into Mike's shuttered face. "You're still
okay with that, aren't you? Her coming to spend the night
at my place, I mean."

"Oh, sure. Yes, of course. So." He gave her a forced
smile. "I'll hear from you then. You've got my office
number?"

"Yes, I do."

They looked at each other. Hally knew she ought to get
going. She had that Italian language class to attend tonight.

But she was struck by how weary he seemed. How somehow sad. Deeply, inconsolably sad.

And she suddenly knew she wasn't going anywhere without him because she simply couldn't bear to just leave him like that.

"Say, are you as hungry as I am?" she asked with what she hoped was a convincing show of artless spontaneity.

Mike frowned as if he wasn't sure and needed to think about it. "Well, now that you mention it," he finally said, "I can't say I remember eating lunch…"

"I know this really nice place," Hally ventured on, deciding to take Mike's vague reply in the affirmative. "Not too loud, not too quiet. Not too far from here."

"Sounds good."

"Angelo's. It's Italian." She peered into his still too somber face. "You do like Italian?"

"These days I like anything as long as it isn't pizza."

"Not even on the menu," Hally assured him. She gestured to his car, still striving to lighten his mood. "Your chariot or mine?"

Mike gave her an odd look. "Are you going to be like this for the rest of the night?"

Hally blinked, taken aback. "Like what?"

"All jolly and cute like a Santa Claus elf."

Hally blinked again, wavering between being hurt and being amused. She opted for being amused and smothered a laugh with her hand. "Too much, huh?"

"Just a bit, yeah." Mike looked into eyes that twinkled with an endearing mix of self-effacing humor. In spite of his depression and the gravity of the situation, he couldn't help but smile back.

Hally didn't think she'd ever seen a more heart-stopping smile on a man. Too bad it vanished almost as quickly as it had appeared. He smiled much too rarely and she found herself regretting that much more than she should as a relatively uninvolved outsider.

This man could easily get to you, her faithful inner voice whispered in her ear.

Only if I let him, Hally silently countered. *Which I certainly won't.*

"Why don't we each drive our own car?" she suggested. That seemed like the perfect way to avoid the intimacy that would be forced upon them by the confines of a car. "And meet at the restaurant. You'd better follow me, though, because I'm lousy at giving directions."

Mike found that hard to believe, but nodded his assent. The way he was feeling right now, he would have followed her anywhere just so he wouldn't have to go home.

Home. He almost laughed. Where exactly was that for him, anyway? Not in Idaho. Not in Saudi Arabia or any of the other countries in which he'd lived for some months, a year, or more, for most of his adult life. And most certainly "home" was not that ugly pink eyesore he shared with Corinne.

He gestured with his hand. "Lead on, McDuff."

Hally pulled a face. "Now who's being cute?"

"Touché." And, incredible though it seemed in view of everything he'd been through that day, as he followed Halloran McKenzie's garish yellow little Bug, he was closer to being at peace than he'd been in a long, long time.

The feeling stayed with him as he pulled into the spot beside her in the small parking lot behind the restaurant. It seemed natural to take Hally's hand as they walked toward the entrance. And it felt comfortable not to speak.

The place smelled good. Lots of garlic, fresh bread and tomato smells. Warmth, both tangible and atmospheric, enveloped Mike as he walked through the door.

"I can see why you like this place," he murmured, bending to Hally's ear so that she could hear him over an accordion player's energetic performance.

"I love everything Italian." Hally turned her head to smile up at Mike and their noses touched. For an instant, they froze, eyes on each other with a startled jolt of awareness, and then they pointedly relaxed.

"But especially the food," Hally said, pretending nonchalance while pulling her suddenly sweaty hand out of his. And as they followed the waiter to their table, she remained excruciatingly aware of Mike close behind her.

"Thank you," they said in unison as the waiter handed them their menus, and exchanged a quick glance of feigned amusement before studying the bill of fare with instant absorption.

For her part, Hally had never been more conscious of anyone in her life. Even with her eyes glued to the pasta selections, she knew exactly what Mike was doing—laying down the menu, looking around, taking a drink of water. She inhaled a carefully controlled breath that she hoped would slow down her heartbeats, which were way off the scale.

Oh, yes, she thought with a touch of despair, this man could definitely get to her.

She cleared her throat. "I think I'll go with the fettuccini," she said to make it seem as though she'd been carefully weighing the selection of entrées instead of reveling in Mike Parker's presence. Closing the menu, she laid it on the table and glanced up.

Right into Gilbert Smith's puzzled visage.

Chapter Five

In retrospect Hally decided she could have handled things better. As it was, she had felt herself flush in an outward betrayal of inner guilt that was as unwelcome as it was unwarranted. She had nothing to feel guilty about. She was having dinner with the parent of one of her students. It was, so to speak, all in the line of duty.

But apparently Gil hadn't bought into that. Probably because it wasn't entirely true. Her interest in Michael Parker had gone beyond the merely professional.

But so had her interest in his daughter, she hastened to point out to herself. They were two people she took an interest in on a humanitarian level. Surely there was nothing sinister or improper in that.

So why had she stammered like some witless nincompoop while introducing the two men to each other?

Gilbert's cool refusal of her lukewarm invitation to join Michael and her had put a damper on the rest of the evening, as far as she was concerned. True, Gil was at the restaurant with his mother, who had never made a secret of the fact that she didn't much care for Hally. If Gil had been even ten years younger than the thirty-six years he wore with such a dignified air of responsibility, Hally was sure Mrs. Smith would have long ago forbidden her son to date Hally. As it was, she and Hally exchanged polite greetings and phony smiles during their infrequent encounters and that was all.

No, the reason the zip had gone out of the evening for Hally—not that there had been a lot of it to start with, given the situation with Corinne—was that seeing Gil next to Mike had made her wonder what in the world she'd ever seen in Gilbert to start with. Had he always been so...old-maidish? So...petulant?

The way he had replied to Hally's inquiry into the state of his cold—"You were obviously too busy with other things to give me a call earlier." *Sniff...*

What kind of thing was that for a man to say?

And that other thing. "I don't suppose you'll be available for our tennis date tomorrow, either?"

Where had that come from? True, until that moment, Hally hadn't thought about their weekly tennis game one way or another. There'd been too much else to think about.

In view of her commitment to Corinne, however, what else could Hally have said but, "Gee, Gil, I'm sorry, but I really won't be."

Which, from Gilbert Smith's perspective, had obviously been the final straw. He had swept Mike a scathing glare and stalked away with nothing more than a churlish, "I guess I'll see you around."

Mike had been quiet throughout the thankfully brief encounter, pretending for the most part to be absorbed in his menu. Hally figured he had to know it by heart by now.

"Sorry if I caused you problems with your boyfriend," he said when Gilbert was out of earshot.

"He's not my boyfriend," Hally said crossly, though as recently as a couple of days ago that was pretty much how she herself had referred to Gil. ''We're colleagues and we, well, we've dated a bit, that's all.''

''He seemed upset, though, to find you here with me.''

''Well, if he is, that's his problem,'' Hally said with a lot more nonchalance than she felt. She didn't like hurting people, least of all people she cared about. Gil was a friend, or, at least, he had been. It saddened her to realize that this perfectly innocent dinner might well have ended that friendship. She decided to speak with Gil tomorrow to straighten things out.

The decision made it possible for her to order and to look forward to her fettuccini dinner once more, but her mood took another nosedive when Gil and his mother passed their table without a word of goodbye or even a glance.

''Here's to you.'' Mike roused her from the doldrums by raising his glass of the Chianti he had ordered for Hally and himself. Forcing a smile, Hally accepted his toast and took a sip as he added, ''And to a successful conclusion of Project Corinne.''

''You came home late last night,'' Hally's mother remarked as Hally stopped in to check on her after lunch the next day. ''Did you have fun?''

''Hardly.'' Hally quickly filled her mother in on the pertinent details. She was glad to find Edith up and about, and to note that the gash and bruise on her head were nicely healing. ''I taught my classes this morning,'' she concluded, ''and will be springing Corinne from jail in about an hour and a half. Bill O'Rourke, by the way, has been most helpful.''

As she had known it would, this brought a dazzling smile to her mother's lips. ''You really like that man, don't you, Mom?''

''Yes.'' Edith's expression turned dreamy. ''He makes me feel...*special* and more feminine than I've felt in a long, long time." She glanced at Hally with a blush on her cheeks. "Does that sound foolish?"

"Not at all." Hally hugged her mother with a rush of affection. "It sounds wonderful, and I'm so happy for you."

"Thank you, darling," Edith said with a loving glance that quickly turned wistful. "I only wish I could be as happy for you."

"Mother." Hally let go of her mother. She picked up her mug and took it to the sink. "Don't start. Okay? I've had a very trying morning."

Edith was instantly concerned. "You do too much, Hally, really you do. You expend too much of yourself on these children."

"Oh, Mother." Hally rinsed her cup and set it in the rack. Drying her hands and tossing the towel aside, she strove to keep impatience out of her tone. "I know you feel that way and I appreciate your concern. But I don't see myself and my life in that light and I wish you'd just leave it alone. Besides, it wasn't one of my students who soured my morning, it was Gil."

"Gil?" Edith repeated, watching with a frown as Hally slumped against the counter and raked both hands through her hair. "Gilbert *Smith?*"

"Only Gil I know," Hally muttered, vexed with herself for sparing the man even one more regret.

"You've quarreled?" Edith asked.

Hally dropped her hands and pushed away from the counter. "Nothing as straightforward as that, I'm afraid. More like he's having himself a good sulk."

Her motions listless, she picked up her handbag. Gilbert had cut her cold when she'd stopped him in the hall that morning, and this rankled. She kissed her mother's cheek and headed for the door. "Don't worry about it."

"But..."

"Later, Mom." Hally closed the door, forestalling fur-

ther questions. She decided it would have been better if
she hadn't said anything to her mother about Gil. Edith
tended to fret; she was eager for Hally to pick a guy and
settle down. Give her a grandchild or two to cuddle.

It was a sore point between them—Hally's adamant
stance against matrimony and the resultant unlikelihood
that there'd ever be a grandchild for Edith to spoil. With
Morgan more than halfway across the country and firmly
allied with James McKenzie, Morgan's six-year-old,
Kenny, was a virtual stranger to his maternal grandmother.
A regrettable circumstance none of the parties involved
had so far been capable of resolving, but which Hally
couldn't see herself making up for by getting married.

She sighed, her spirits in the dumps. They plunged even
lower when she saw that she had another flat tire. This
time on the other side. She supposed buying a set of new
ones could no longer be avoided.

The police station was no place for anyone with a headache. After getting a cab to Mike's house, Hally and Mike
had driven there in his car. Hally's head ached and her
eyes burned. Her thoughts kept wanting to stray.

She hadn't spent much time at the Parker house, just
long enough for Mike to change clothes and get ready. She
had gone and sat on the sofa in the living room—at Mike's
insistence, with a can of diet soda in her hands. She'd
sipped it and thought how strangely intimate it seemed to
be sitting just one not-quite-closed door away from a man
who was a relative stranger and currently taking his clothes
off. She could hear him doing it; could hear one foot
thump on the floor as he lifted the other to get out of or
into his pants. She could hear closet doors and drawers
opening and closing. And then water running in the bath-
room.

And all of this activity was punctuated by a disjointed
conversation carried on in semi-raised voices.

Actually, it wasn't a conversation so much as a question-and-answer session. With Mike asking the questions and Hally, rather pensively, answering.

Questions like, "So you're Long Beach born and raised, huh?"

"Uh-huh." Hally recalled having told him she was a California native the previous day when that…that *neighbor* had been at the house. Glancing around as they chatted, she tried to determine why the room seemed so lackluster in spite of the tasteful furniture. "But I did go away to college."

"U.C.L.A.?"

"Yes. Initially." Her eyes fell on a silver framed photo of a woman standing beside a horse. "I did postgraduate studies at Stanford."

"Been married, have you?"

"Nope." Curiosity made Hally get up from the couch and walk over to the photo. It and an ormolu clock were the sole occupants of an otherwise empty shelf in a cherry-wood bookcase the lovely patina of which was barely discernible under a layer of dust. Obviously neither of the two Parkers was into dusting furniture.

"The way you say that," Mike called from the other room, "sounds like you've got something against it."

"I don't." Hally studied the picture. Clearly, this was Corinne's mother. A pretty woman, not much older than her own thirty-two years. Dark hair, laughing eyes and, in tight jeans and a T-shirt, showing off the well-toned body of an equestrienne.

No thigh worries there, Hally thought with an inward grimace at this obsession of hers. Aloud she fleshed out her reply by adding, "As long as someone else does the marrying."

"I take it you got burned." Mike closed the bedroom door and came to stand next to her. He was dressed in khaki slacks and a light blue cotton sweater.

"Maybe," Hally said evasively, furtively inhaling the scent of freshly laundered clothes and crisp aftershave that emanated from him as he moved. Unnerved because she found his proximity disturbing, she set the picture down and took a step back. "Though from the little I've heard about you and—Rebecca, isn't it?—I'd say it's obvious *you* didn't. She was very lovely."

"Yes, she was." Mike's clipped tone made it clear he didn't want to discuss his deceased wife. Or so Hally thought.

And so she was surprised when, with a pensive sort of reluctance, he added, "But, you know, I'm not sure our marriage would have lasted even if she'd lived. Certainly not without some serious counseling. More and more, those last couple of years, Becky and I'd be like strangers whenever I came home on leave. Pretending we weren't was very stressful for us both. We fought a lot."

"Was Corinne aware of this?"

"I'd say so. Yes." Mike took a deep breath and noisily expelled it. He glanced down at his hands, toying with his keys. He was telling Hally things he had never told anyone. Things he wasn't proud of. Feelings he had buried. He knew why, of course—to help Hally help Cory.

Or was there another reason? He glanced at the woman, noting her expression of concern, of genuine interest. She was an empathetic listener, which made her easy to talk to. To be with.

And she wasn't too hard on the eyes, either, which made her a pleasure to be seen with.

Appalled by that errant observation, Mike immediately chastised himself with an impatient, *Grow up, Parker. That kind of sophomoric lusting hardly does you credit and is an insult to the woman.*

"I hate to admit it," he said, moving away to put some space between Hally and himself, "but many times the tension got thick enough to cut with a knife. And some of our...disagreements got pretty loud.''

"Hmm." Hally's professional interest overrode the personal one she'd been trying to convince herself didn't exist. "My guess is your daughter heard and observed more than you think. Internalizing, and probably misinterpreting much of what was going on could very well be the reason she's so angry.''

She glanced at her watch, noted that it was time to get going, and went to get her purse off the couch. "Was divorce ever mentioned in the course of these... confrontations?''

"Once." Mike held the door open so Hally could precede him out of the house. "Shortly before Rebecca found out she had...um, cancer...''

As always, he choked on the word, and the mixture of grief and regret that came with it. Ovarian cancer had claimed Becky all too soon, all too swiftly. Whatever the differences and estrangement their too long and too frequent separations had caused, she'd been his first love. And he wished with all his heart that she could have lived a long and happy life. With or without him in it.

"She was dead six months later," he said gruffly, not looking at Hally who had stopped in front of him in the doorway and was listening with her heart in her throat. "I never saw her alive again.''

"I'm so sorry." Hally impulsively touched his arm. "It must've been hell.''

"Yeah." Mike looked down at her fingers on his sleeve, then up into her face with an expression Hally couldn't begin to define. It made her feel funny, though, and she quickly took back her hand.

"It *was* hell," he said. "At least until the day before yesterday....''

Most people would consider a night in prison a pretty hellish experience, too. Not so, by all outward appearances, Corinne Parker.

She strolled out of the police station with a sequoia-size chip on her shoulder and fairly bristling with attitude. She didn't spare her father more than a contemptuous glance. Everything about her made it clear she didn't buy his performance with Sergeant O'Rourke. The good sergeant had, as previously agreed, acted hard-nosed about Corinne's so-called early release. And Mike had—in Hally's opinion—been most convincing as his daughter's champion.

"I'm taking you home with me for the night," Hally informed the girl out on the sidewalk. Her head still pounding, she didn't even try to be cordial.

Let her thank her lucky stars I'm speaking to her at all, was about how Hally felt just then. She pointedly ignored Corinne's nonverbal response of an apathetic shrug. She did exchange a glance with Mike behind Corinne's back, however, prior to getting into the cab Mike had called to take them to Hally's. The despair and frustration that darkened his eyes managed to drag from her an attempted smile of sympathy and reassurance.

"We'll see you at the court hearing tomorrow morning," she said. "Promptly at ten."

"Ten," Mike repeated, handing Hally the small duffel he had packed for Corinne. Though it contained, among other things, a change of clothes and toiletries, Corinne would probably spurn his choice of outfits. He wouldn't be surprised to see her in court tomorrow wearing the same ratty denim overalls, black T-shirt and army surplus boots she had on today.

"Well, have fun," he added lamely as Hally and his daughter got into the taxi.

"Thanks," Hally said.

Corinne just wordlessly glared up at him before turning to Hally with a smirk. "Good," she said. "He's really ticked."

"And this pleases you?" As they pulled away from the curb, Hally caught a glimpse of Mike. He was walking toward his car with a decidedly dejected air. Her heart contracted and she vowed she would help this man, come hell or high water. "Why?" she asked coolly.

"Why not?" Corinne predictably snapped. She turned her face away and said, "He gets his kicks tormenting me. Now I'm tormenting him."

"'Tormenting'?" Hally was too well acquainted with teenage theatrics and exaggeration to give the word credence in a literal sense. "And just how does your father *torment* you, Corinne?"

"Well." Corinne favored Hally with a glance that clearly asked, *Why do I even have to talk to you?* "Aside from the fact that he's in my face over every little fart, he got me stuck into prison, didn't he?"

"Actually, no," Hally said calmly, crossing her legs. "*I* got you 'stuck into prison.' *He* got you out. Against my better judgment, I might add."

Hally uttered the lie without compunction. Much better the girl should despise her teacher than her father. Who knew better than she the pain that was caused by despising one's dad?

"You're a truant, Corinne. And tomorrow's hearing might very well land you back behind the bars of a juvenile detention facility unless *I* testify that you will mend your ways."

Corinne snorted derisively. She raked Hally with a hostile glance before once again turning her face toward the window in the passenger door.

Hally made no effort to break the pulsing silence that followed her words. In her opinion, the ball was now in Corinne's court. They had driven several miles and were almost at the duplex when the girl finally spoke.

"What'm I s'posed to do at your house, anyway?" she asked in a sullen tone.

"Oh, I dunno." Chalking one up for Mike's side because she considered outsilencing the girl a small victory, Hally scooped up her purse as the cab swung into her driveway. She opened her door, blithely saying, "We'll think of something."

Corinne muttered an indistinct response that Hally, paying the driver, decided was just as well she hadn't been able to catch. The girl's scowl and pulled-down corners of the mouth left her with no doubt the words had not been an expression of joy.

As she followed Hally up the steps to the front door, Corinne's footsteps dragged as though she were being led to the gallows. Hally unlocked and threw open the door and almost lost her balance as a large, gray shadow streaked between her legs into the house ahead of them.

"Chaucer McKenzie!" Hally cried, tottering because she'd been too preoccupied today to be mindful of what was, after all, the cat's usual mode of entry, "You silly cat! One of these day's you'll make me break my neck!"

Steadying herself on the doorjamb, she scowled down at the cat who was meowing loudly and unapologetically while rubbing his sides against her legs.

A small noise from just behind her drew Hally's attention back to her guest. Turning her head, she saw Corinne Parker sinking down to her knees, beckoning to Chaucer with outstretched hands. "Here, kitty-cat," she called softly.

And so tenderly, Hally caught her breath in surprise. Surprise that turned swiftly to utter amazement as the crotchety old tomcat, who made friends with no one, walked without hesitation into the girl's waiting arms and promptly turned into a lump of purring putty.

Chapter Six

"Did you know your daughter loved cats?" Hally asked Mike the moment she got him alone. She had gotten a sub for her morning classes and met him at the courthouse. The hearing was over. It had lasted less than an hour. Most of the kids, Corinne included, had been remanded into the custody of their parents or legal guardians. They were given a three-month probationary period during which they were to observe a curfew of no later than 10:00 p.m. They'd also had to listen to a lengthy lecture on the disastrous consequences of mob behavior, rock concerts in general and this past canceled one in particular, and were sent on their way with a stern reminder to stay on the straight and narrow. A few, the instigators of the near riot, were bound over for trial at a later date.

The parents present, too, had been sternly admonished by the fire-breathing judge to fulfill their responsibilities to their children and society by exercising sufficient control over their offspring to prevent another visit to her courtroom. She would hold them personally responsible, the judge had said, if she had to clap eyes on any of them ever again.

Corinne, free, had gone to the ladies' room, leaving Hally and Mike on a bench in the corridor to wait for her. She had been markedly subdued prior to the hearing and, to Mike, had looked astonishingly and delightfully wholesome and pretty in a narrow little black skirt, black tights and black-and-white striped top. All of them newly purchased and picked out, with Hally's help, by Corinne herself. Or so Halloran had earlier confided. He now owed this miracle of a woman—as he was beginning to think of her—eighty-seven dollars, but he considered it money well spent.

Hally had also seen to it that Corinne wore a minimum of makeup and that her impossible hair was decently combed.

Mike was profoundly grateful, but as to the question about cats.... He furrowed his brow. "I guess I didn't. I mean, there've always been cats around my folks' house. And now that you mention it, Becky kept a couple of 'em, too..."

"They were Corinne's." Hally shifted on the hard wooden bench, crossing her legs and thus giving Mike a much appreciated view of some very shapely ankles and calves. "Their names are Figaro and Shadow. Fig's five, Shadow's three, and both of them are now at your parents' house."

"You mean to tell me Cory related all of that to you in one overnight visit?" Hurt and yes, dammit, jealousy made the question come out much more harshly than Mike had intended. He hadn't meant for his voice to sound harsh at all, merely surprised. But to think he hadn't had a clue! "She actually *volunteered* all that to you?"

"Well, I certainly didn't have her up against a wall with a gun to her head," Hally quipped. She decided to ignore his somewhat strident tone because she knew how emotionally battered he was feeling.

"We did quite a fair amount of talking, as a matter of fact," she went on, neglecting to mention the nerve-racking hours of truculent silence and monosyllabic replies that had preceded the eventual slight thaw. "Once she decided to toss that giant chip off her shoulder."

She tugged her skirt down, shrugging in response to Mike's question—unvoiced, but most clearly conveyed by his unblinking stare and blackest black scowl. "Psych 101, remember?"

She had hoped it would make him smile, having his own remark from four—only four?—days ago tossed back at him like this. She realized he was not in a mood for humor—and, to be honest, couldn't blame him—when his scowl only got blacker.

"Sorry," she said. "I didn't mean to be flippant. But the fact is I *am* a counselor and I do have a degree in psychology. Not to mention that I've been trained to draw these kids out. For the most part all it takes is time and a bit of patience."

"Time and patience." Mike leaned forward, propping his elbows on his spread knees. He stared straight ahead with a sigh. "You told me once before that's what it takes." He sliced her a sideways glance. "Remember?"

"Oh, yes." Hally smiled. "Our first meeting."

"Exactly." He stared down at his hands. They were dangling between his legs, but he kept flexing and unflexing his fingers as though doing warm-up exercises before a session at the piano.

Watching his hands, Hally marveled again at their size, and wondered if he played a musical instrument. If not that, then surely he had played basketball in high school.

"So what did I turn around and do?" he asked rhetorically, and with so much feeling in his voice that Hally felt ashamed of her wandering thoughts, "when I finally got her home from that dad-blasted concert fiasco and should have practiced a bit of forbearance? I practically took her head off about a few measly bucks.''

''One hundred and thirty *stolen* bucks,'' Hally reminded him acerbically, ''is hardly what I would call measly. And,'' she consoled when he continued to stare grimly down at his hands, ''your little darling had just put you through one heck of an emotional wringer.

''So, don't be so hard on yourself, Mr. Michael J. Parker.''

He gave her look that said, *Easy for you to say.* ''I've done everything wrong.''

''You did the best you knew how,'' Hally countered. ''That's all anyone can expect a parent to do.''

Oh, really? And does this generous concession of yours apply to your own parents, too? Distressed by this inner jeer, Hally jumped to her feet with an inarticulate little sound.

Startled out of his contemplation of the floor and instantly concerned, Mike, too, surged off the bench. He put a hand on Hally's shoulder and gently forced her to turn around. ''What?'' He searched her face. It looked stricken. ''What's the matter?''

''I'm sorry,'' she frustrated him by evading with an embarrassed little laugh. ''It's nothing.''

''You're upset.'' And it hardly took a course of Psych 101 to know people didn't get upset from nothing. He looked at her, waiting.

But Hally only shook her head and insisted, ''It's nothing. Really. A light went on, that's all.''

She clearly expected this cryptic statement to end the matter, but when he continued to study her features for signs of stress, she added an apologetic, ''It's something private. I'm sorry.''

''There's nothing to be sorry for,'' Mike said a little stiffly. He knew it was probably unreasonable of him, but couldn't help feeling a stab of resentment at her reticence. After all, his life was an open book, while her life...

Should be none of my damned business, he sternly reminded himself. It wasn't as if she were prying into his affairs out of idle curiosity.

"Well, anyway," Hally said by way of closing the subject. Unaware though she was of Mike's self-talk, she had just given herself a similar one on the subject of professional conduct and was now all set to keep her focus where it belonged—on Michael Parker's troubles.

As to the situation with her father—well, maybe the time had come for some plain talk with Edith.

"As far's Corinne is concerned," she said to Mike. "You're now aware of what it takes. And you're now willing to follow up on that. It's a start."

"I guess."

"Definitely," Hally said firmly. "But I meant to ask you—" She glanced in the direction of the rest room. Corinne was nowhere to be seen, no doubt taking her time and delighting in the fact that she was making the adults wait. "Would you object to my having Corinne come over to my house the next couple of Saturdays? I'll be working with her at school, too, of course, but I think she'd really benefit from some extra time with me."

"Benefit how?" Mike demanded, startling her. She had fully expected him to readily go along with her plans and had asked only as a matter of form.

"Well." She scrambled to give some credible reasons— of which there were many, of course—but wouldn't you know all she could think of to say was, "There's the cat, for one thing."

"I can get her a cat." Mike wasn't sure why he was being difficult. He knew he should be grateful to Hally for all she had done and was offering to do. It had to be quite a sacrifice, giving up her Saturdays.

"Do you have all your problem students over to the house?"

"Well, no, but..." Hally struggled to keep her pique over what she interpreted as Mike's distrust of her motives from coloring her voice. "It just so happens that Corinne is...well, she's not your run-of-the-mill troubled student."

"Oh?" Mike was tempted to add, *Because of me?* But he immediately doused this ridiculous flare up of male ego. "And why's that?"

"I don't know..." She reminds me of me at that age, Hally thought. All that anger and angst....

Somehow this seemed like too personal a thing to confide, however, until it struck her that she owed this man, this father, at least a glimpse of something personal so that he might realize she had no ulterior motives. And so that he could trust her. After all, with so many deviants running loose in the world, he had a right and a duty to be cautious. Even if it wasn't very flattering to her.

She took a breath and reversed her previous reply. "Actually I do know," she said. She went on to briefly fill him in on the trauma and turmoil of her own teenage years—the absentee, workaholic, perfectionist father whom she couldn't seem to please on those rare occasions when he was at home. She told of how she'd yearned for his love and approval, but had never seemed quite good enough, smart enough, pretty enough for him.

"At the time," she concluded, "I was helped a great deal by talks with my mother. Mom was always an excellent listener. I'm told it's a trait I've inherited."

"I guess I can vouch for that," Mike conceded a little awkwardly. He appreciated Hally's candor about her past but could think of no way to convey that to her.

That was one of his biggest problems, he groused silently, this inability of his to vocalize what was in his heart. Give him a business problem to solve, a speech to make, or a presentation—no sweat. But put him up against the female mind or anything personal and emotional and he bombed big-time. "You, uh, you've been great."

"If you truly believe that," Hally said, warmed all out of proportion by his, at best, tepid praise, "then please do allow Corinne to bend my ear for a couple of weeks. She needs to talk out her anger with a sympathetic but objective outsider before she's able to rationally talk it out with you."

"I suppose that does make sense."

"But you're not happy about it," Hally observed as his grudging voice faded into an obviously doubtful silence. "You still don't trust me to know what I'm doing, is that it?"

"No, that's not it," Mike denied. He knew he sounded angry, but what he was, was scared. And he hated having to admit it. "The thing is, the problems Cory and I are having stem from her too strong attachment to her mother and her estrangement from me. What if she fixates on you now instead of—"

"Oh, Mike." With understanding came instant empathy. If she'd dared give in to her impulse, Hally would have reached out and smoothed the worry lines off his brow. Poor man, he was feeling so obviously vulnerable to further hurt and rejection.

She contented herself with touching the sleeve of the natty navy blue blazer he wore with gray flannel slacks. "She won't," she assured him earnestly. "Simply because I would never let it come to that. Her relationship with you will be the main focus of our conversations.

"Trust me," she added quietly, holding his gaze as he looked into her eyes. "Please, Mike..."

"Well, this is cozy," Corinne drawled sarcastically, startling the adults.

Hally guiltily snatched back her hand, then chided herself for overreacting as she and Mike swung around to the girl who stood with her hip cocked and arms folded. She had used the time in the ladies' room to gel her hair once again into spikes and to apply the layers of makeup that turned her face into a younger version of Lily Munster.

She was regarding her father and Hally with poorly feigned mockery and indifference. "You got the hots for my dad, Ms. McKenzie?"

Mike instantly went rigid with outrage. He drew breath for a harsh reprimand, but choked it back when Hally discreetly nudged his foot.

"Corinne," she said, taking the girl by the arm and steering her inexorably toward the exit. "Just this once we'll pretend you didn't say what you just said, shall we?"

Hally kept her voice carefully low and even, though inwardly she was quivering with appalled reaction. Mostly because the girl's tasteless cheap shot had come uncomfortably close to the mark. She added, "Unless, of course, you'd like to apologize to your father and me?"

"Pfff…" Corinne tried to extricate herself from Hally's hold.

Hally's fingers tightened. "Give it up, Corinne," she said pleasantly. "Over the next few weeks at least, you and I are going to become bosom buddies."

"Meaning what?" Corinne snapped. She would no doubt have bitten off her tongue had she known how pleased and encouraged Hally was by this albeit belligerent show of curiosity. It proved what she'd already suspected—more than anything the girl's churlishness was a lonely and bewildered child's cry for help.

"Meaning you'll be spending a whole lot of time with me," Hally almost cheerfully told her. "Both in school and out."

"Really?" This time there was an unmistakable note of interest in Corinne's tone, which she immediately tried to nullify, of course. "I s'pose you'll have me locked up again if I decide to split."

Hally shrugged. "You heard what the judge said—cur-

few and supervision. Both your father and I intend to abide
by that edict.''

"You mean I've gotta spend time with *him,* too?''

Hally realized with a flare of annoyance that Corinne
had deliberately waited to ask that question till Mike was
within earshot. Her heart bled for him, for even though his
facial expression remained carefully controlled, he had
blanched. The girl really was being a first-class stinker.

For the first time it occurred to Hally to wonder if Rebecca Parker, intentionally or through carelessness, might
not have fueled her daughter's animosity toward Mike.

Meanwhile, at a loss as to how to tactfully respond to
the girl's rude question, Hally thought it best to simply
ignore it. She addressed Mike. "Why don't I take Corinne
to school with me now and let you get back to your office?''

Her tire fixed, she was independently mobile again. This
time, hopefully, for more than just a couple of days.
"We've each got several classes yet this afternoon.''

"Well. It's almost noon.'' Mike was trying to inject an
upbeat note into his voice. It wasn't easy. He was feeling
emotionally battered and weary to the bone. "How about
I buy you ladies some lunch first?''

Hally's, "That's awfully nice of you but,'' coincided
with Corinne's muttered, "Yuk.''

Again pretending deafness—and attempting with a
pleading look to convince Mike to do the same—Hally
finished the refusal she'd begun to make. "We'd really
better get going. We'll grab a burger en route and make it
in time for fifth period.

"Right, Corinne?'' she brightly prompted the sullen girl.

Corinne stared into the distance, the picture of boredom.
"Yeah. Sure. Whatever.''

Hally turned to Mike and rolled her eyes. *I'm sorry,* she
mouthed, fervently wishing there was something she could
do or say to bolster his visibly flagging morale. But noth-

ing helpful came to mind and so she said, a bit lamely, "You'll pick her up after school as planned?"

Mike glanced at his daughter's averted face. His lips compressed as he asked himself, *Am I crazy to put store in this woman's promise to turn my daughter around? To hope my child will come to love me?*

A month, he promised himself. He'd give it—her—a month. And if he didn't see an improvement in Cory's attitude after that time he'd do what he'd been all set to do already, return her to Idaho. His folks would be back from their cruise by then, too.

"I'll be there," he said, both irked as well as warmed by the evident empathy on Halloran McKenzie's face.

He was a take-charge kind of man. Always had been, though by no means in a chauvinistic kind of way. He'd just always been a leader, and now to be cast in the role of follower was difficult for him.

Until he reminded himself that the course of rehabilitating Corinne on which Halloran McKenzie had embarked was an uncharted one for him. And that only a stupid man would venture unguided into the unknown.

It was five-thirty on Saturday evening. Mike had been told to pick Corinne up at six, but after being at lose ends all day he didn't think it would matter if he came a bit early.

He surely was one crazy guy, he'd wryly reflected at odd moments throughout the day. To be missing a daughter who, when around, gave him nothing but grief. The past several days since the hearing had seen little improvement in their relationship. At best, they hadn't yelled at each other. But only because they'd taken pains to give one another a wide berth.

By all accounts the school counseling session had been positive. Cory had not only *not* attempted to skip school, she'd had her assignments done, as well. This from Hally

McKenzie since, heaven forbid, Cory should deign to speak to him in anything but monosyllables.

"Your daughter has a brain," Hally had told Mike with a tone of surprise.

This hadn't been news to him, of course. In Idaho, Cory had always been on the honor roll. He supposed he should feel heartened by the fact that she was willing to apply herself once again.

"Hello!" After getting no response the first time, Mike rapped a bit more forcefully on the frame of the locked screen door of Halloran McKenzie's house. He knew he was at the right place since he'd dropped Cory off here this morning. He stuck his face against the screen and peered into the murky twilight within. "Anybody home?"

"Meow."

"Hel-lo." Mike lowered his gaze and encountered the menacing stare of a huge gray cat. It sat on the other side of the screened door, swishing its tail. "So you're the cat."

"His name is Chaucer." Hally's voice come from behind and Mike swung around to find her standing on the path in front of the steps.

"Hi," she greeted with a smile that warmed him a whole lot more than it probably should, and made him glad he had Corinne as a reason to see more of this woman. "I thought I heard a car."

"That's some cat," Mike said, unable to take his eyes off her face as he walked down the steps toward her. "He looked ready to tear me to pieces if I'd dared open the door."

"Bluster, that's all it is." Hally wondered if she had dirt on her face, Mike was staring at her so hard. She wished she could smoothen her hair. Disconcerted for no reason she cared to dwell on, she glanced down at her wrist to check the time, remembered she wasn't wearing a watch and frowned up at Mike. "Are you early? Do you have plans? Corinne's with my mother, but—"

No, no." Mike hoped he didn't come across as gauche as he unaccountably felt. "No particular plans. I... Well, to tell you the truth, I was at loose ends. But if I'm interrupting—"

' Heavens, no." Hally held up her dirt-encrusted hands. "I was gardening, that's all. Come on, I'll show you."

Hally retraced her steps. She assumed—correctly—that Mike would follow.

' You don't believe in gloves?" he asked.

They get in the way." Hally shrugged. "Besides, I like to dig in and feel the earth."

Must be hell on your manicure." Becky had worn gloves for even the smallest household task. Her hands had been one of her few vanities. And they had been beautiful hands.

But, Mike shocked himself by inwardly observing, they'd never turned him on the way the laughing glance Hally McKenzie tossed him did as she quipped, "What manicure? You're looking at the only woman in the entire world who can't even keep acrylic nails from breaking."

She seemed so unaffected by something Rebecca would surely have considered a calamity that Mike was utterly charmed.

"So how'd it go with Cory?" he asked while his eyes latched onto the gentle sway of her hips. They flared from a surprisingly narrow waist in a generous curve that was exactly the way a woman's hips should flare, as far as he was concerned. "She give you any grief?"

"No grief. We're making progress. She adores my mom."

Small wonder, if she's anything like you....

"That's great." Mike cleared his throat. It had gone tight from the alluring vista in front of him. Such legs the woman had. And the way those short-shorts hugged her derriere....

"By any chance are you a cyclist?" he heard himself

PLAY
SILHOUETTE'S

LUCKY HEARTS GAME

AND YOU GET

★ **FREE BOOKS**

★ **A FREE GIFT**

★ **AND MUCH MORE**

TURN THE PAGE AND
DEAL YOURSELF IN

PLAY "LUCKY HEARTS" AND GET . . .

★ **Exciting Silhouette Romance™ novels—FREE**

★ **PLUS a beautiful Cherub Magnet—FREE**

THEN CONTINUE YOUR LUCKY STREAK WITH A SWEETHEART OF A DEAL

1. Play Lucky Hearts as instructed on the opposite page.
2. Send back this card and you'll receive brand-new Silhouette Romance™ novels. These books have a cover price of $3.25 each, but they are yours to keep absolutely free.
3. There's no catch. You're under no obligation to buy anything. We charge nothing — ZERO — for your first shipment. And you don't have to make any minimum number of purchases — not even one!
4. The fact is thousands of readers enjoy receiving books by mail from the Silhouette Reader Service. They like the convenience of home delivery…they like getting the best new novels months before they're available in stores…and they love our discount prices!
5. We hope that after receiving your free books you'll want to remain a subscriber. But the choice is yours — to continue or cancel, anytime at all! So why not take us up on our invitation, with no risk of any kind. You'll be glad you did!

DETACH AND MAIL CARD TODAY

SILHOUETTE'S

*With a coin—
scratch off
the silver card and
check below to see
what we have for you.*

215 CIS CCN9 **(U-SIL-R-10/97)**

YES! I have scratched off the silver card. Please send me all the free books and gift for which I qualify. I understand that I am under no obligation to purchase any books, as explained on the back and on the opposite page.

NAME

_____

ADDRESS   APT.

_____

CITY   STATE   ZIP

Twenty-one gets you 4 free books, and a free Cherub Magnet

Twenty gets you 4 free books

Nineteen gets you 3 free books

Eighteen gets you 2 free books

ask. And inwardly groaned as he realized that the question betrayed where his eyes had been roaming. "I mean, your legs are so darned…"

Shapely and well toned, he'd meant to say, only to d cide that was way too personal. "Muscular."

Oh, God. Mike closed his eyes. Had he really said "muscular"? Mr. Smooth, that was him, he thought, and felt like a perfect jerk when Hally stopped walking and faced him with a definite blush staining her cheeks. Clearly, he'd embarrassed her.

In truth, Hally was more than embarrassed, she was aghast. She hadn't considered that by preceding Mike Parker up the path to her backyard she'd be presenting him with a view of her worst features—her hips and thighs!

Muscular legs, indeed! *Fat* legs was surely what he'd been too polite to say, but must certainly have been thinking.

"Actually, I in-line skate," she said, feigning blithe unselfconsciousness, though badly, judging by Mike Parker's obvious discomfiture. Knowing she was the cause of it made her feel even worse.

She redoubled her efforts to appear matter-of-fact and blasé. "But I'm also enrolled in an aerobics class to pare down that darned gluteus maximus."

She dared raise her eyes to his at last. And was suffused by a wave of heat from the fire that flared there as he murmured, "Nothing wrong with it that I can see."

Wow. Hally's knees quaked and her heart began to race as Mike relentlessly held her gaze. And though he spoke not another word, the expression in his eyes made it crystal clear that she was a woman who was passionately desired by this man.

Mercy. Hally groped behind her with her hand and pressed it against the wall of the house for support. She swallowed, and would have loved to moisten her suddenly parched lips. But she didn't dare move, didn't dare to blink as much as a lash lest the motion break the spell of the moment.

Never had a man looked at her as Michael J. Parker was looking at her—like a starving man at a smorgasbord. She wanted to savor this magical moment before reality intruded in one way or another, as it surely must.

"Mike?" She breathed his name, a shivery, questioning sigh.

He took a step toward her.

Hally parted her lips in anticipation.

And closed them again with a snap. *What in the world am I doing?*

She shook her head. "Don't."

Mike froze, his eyes still riveted on her face. It had blanched, and he realized, appalled, that he'd been about to make a pass at his daughter's teacher. And that the woman looked terrified.

"I'm so sorry." He stepped back. He speared rigid fingers into his hair and released the pent-up breath that was causing quite a pain in his chest. "I didn't mean—"

"Oh, please. Don't." Hally held up a hand and barely stopped herself from touching him. "Please don't apologize. It's me. I—"

"Like hell," Mike growled, chagrined. "I had no call to get personal, to say what I did. You've been nothing but generous and kind—"

"And you've been nothing but courteous," Hally interrupted crossly because, to her consternation, she found his need to apologize irritating in the extreme. Especially since part of her wished he hadn't let her stop him.

Stop him from doing what, exactly?

Silly question, since she knew without a doubt that Mike had been about to kiss her.

Heady thought. Wondrous feelings. Total disaster! Hally sternly reminded herself that she had goals. Italy. Sabbatical. Noninvolvement with the opposite sex.

Not to mention that starting something with Mike would put the death knell on anything they hoped to accomplish with Corinne.

Sighing, Hally decided to be totally up front. "Look, Mike," she said. "It isn't that I'm not attracted to you. I am."

"I know."

That set her back a pace. She stared at him, waiting to feel offended, outraged. Such arrogance...

Except it wasn't arrogance at all, Hally thought as her gaze once more meshed with his. It was the truth. He knew it. And she knew it. Perhaps that was a kind of arrogance. Maybe it should have offended her. But it didn't.

What it did do was give her the courage to say back to him what she never would have even conceived of saying to any man before. "And you're attracted to me."

"Like steel to a magnet," Mike wryly conceded, though he wasn't sure where Hally was going with this. Clearly, though, her declaration had not been meant as a come-on, but more like the opposite.

"I take it that isn't good," he observed, catching the shadows of regret lurking in her expressive eyes.

"It's worse than no good," Hally admitted. "It's terrible. And impossible."

Michael nodded, lips compressed. "Corinne?"

"Among other things." Hally averted her eyes.

"Like that Smith guy, for instance?" Mike couldn't keep himself from asking.

And was a bit put out when Hally burst out in a laugh. "Gil?" She waved her hand as though swatting at a pesky fly. "Lord, no. We're friends. Or were."

She began walking again, forgetting all about not wanting to present Mike with her backside. "He hasn't spoken to me since he saw us together at the restaurant."

"Hey, I'm sorry." Mike wasn't, but figured that in situations such as this candor was a good thing only within reason. "Maybe if I talked to him..."

"Forget it. Behold—" Hally stopped at a low fence enclosing a large plot of soil. She looked at it with pride and determinedly changed the subject. "My vegetable patch."

Mike glanced at the plot, then back at Hally. Though he would have preferred sticking to their previous topic of conversation, he followed her lead and pretended interest by raising his brows. "So where's the vegetables?"

"Over there." Hally pointed to a laundry line where bunches of onions had been hung to dry in the sun. "Best crop I've had in years."

"Onions?" Mike's eyebrows climbed higher. "That's all you grow?"

"No. But that's all they leave me," Hally explained, deadpan. She had long since resigned herself to sharing the land with whatever critters had staked out a prior claim.

"'They'?" Michael asked. "They who?"

Hally was enjoying herself. "Why, the rabbits, of course."

"The 'rabbits'?"

"Sure." Hally had to bite her cheek to keep from laughing at Michael's bewildered expression. Poor man, he was much too serious most of the time. "They seem to hate onions." She spread her hands. "But then, so do I."

She caught his uncertain expression and burst out laughing. After a fractional hesitation, Mike began to chuckle.

"Why, Ms. McKenzie," he said, shaking a finger with mock reproval, "I do believe you're a bit of a brat."

Chapter Seven

"**I** could have told you that." As the new voice intruded into their tête-à-tête, Mike took a step away from Hally who, after another amused glance at him, greeted the woman cheerily.

"Hi, Mom. You two done for the day?"

"I think so, yes." Edith turned intrigued eyes to Mike. "You're Corinne's father."

"Guilty." With a grin, he offered his hand. "Mike Parker."

"Your daughter looks like you." She took his hand with left one, which reminded him that she'd recently been injured. Her grip was surprisingly strong, though, for a woman who was slender almost to the point of frailty. "I'm Edith Halloran."

"A pleasure." *Edith Halloran.* Mike marveled that he hadn't made the connection before. Halloran was not exactly a commonplace kind of name, after all. "My mother has several of your pieces," he said.

"Really?" More pleased than Mike would have figured an artist of her renown would be on hearing something like that, Edith turned to Corinne who had lagged behind. "You didn't tell me your grandmother had some of my art," she said, drawing the visibly reluctant girl into their circle.

"I didn't know she did." Corinne shot her father a glare as though she thought he had deliberately put her in a bad light. "Where exactly does she have them, Dad?"

"Well..." Pretending Corinne's question hadn't been an obvious attempt to put him on the spot, Mike kept his voice even. "For starters there are those two stained glass panels on either side of the front door." He glanced at Edith. "My mother's name is Iris and there's a single iris in the center of each of the panels."

"Oh, but how delightful." Edith pressed her clasped hands to her lips, as artlessly pleased and excited as a child who'd been given a gift. "I remember them exactly because they were one of my first custom orders." She frowned, hand to brow. "I probably should recall the name of the firm who commissioned the pieces. I'm hopeless when it comes to the business end of things...some architectural firm..."

"McManus and Associates," Mike supplied, restoring Edith's beaming smile.

"That's right. McManus. Remember, darling?" she said to Hally who'd been watching and listening and feeling quite pleased with how well everyone seemed to be hitting it off. "Those Tiffany-style lamps and fixtures?"

Hally didn't, but knew better than to say so outright. Edith firmly expected everyone who knew her, but especially her own family, to take as much proprietary pride in each piece of her work as she did.

And so Hally let a noncommittal "Hmm," serve as her reply, knowing Edith would choose that to mean yes. As her eyes met Mike's, however, the expression of amusement in his made it clear she hadn't fooled him. She blushed guiltily and he winked at her before turning his full attention back to Edith.

Hally followed suit, but only inasmuch as that she physically turned her head in her mother's direction. Her emotional awareness remained centered on Mike Parker in a way that deeply disturbed her, especially since she seemed unable to do anything about it. It stemmed from the way he'd looked at her earlier, of course, when he'd caught her hand and the air between them had seemed to crackle with that peculiar kind of tension.

He'd wanted to kiss her. And, foolishly, for a moment there she had hoped with every fiber of her being that he would. They shared an attraction. They'd even admitted it.

And, she reminded herself sternly, they'd agreed that it just wouldn't do to do anything about it.

Because that decision seemed now to be causing her to feel an aching sense of loss, Hally forced herself to focus on Corinne who stood with her head bent, watching the toe of her black platform pump nudge a pebble. The girl had seemingly overnight gone from grunge to retro dressing, which Hally considered a vast improvement.

At the moment, Corinne was clearly resentful and embarrassed as Mike told Edith his mother owned two of those Tiffanys, too.

"One of them's in the game room," he was elaborating for his daughter's benefit. "Above Grandpa's pool table."

"Oh, yeah," Corinne mumbled. She didn't need to raise her head for the adults to recognize that she was embarrassed and didn't like it. Her tone was grudging, sullen, the kind of tone teenagers everywhere used to indicate extreme boredom so that their real feelings wouldn't be detected. "I guess I didn't know..."

"And there's no reason in the world why you should," Edith assured her, cheerfully overlooking the truculent tone. "When you looked at those pieces in your grandmother's house, you didn't know me and you certainly

didn't know anything about stained-glass art. Or recognize
the fact that you have a very special talent.''

"Talent?'' Mike shifted a glance of startled inquiry
from Edith's serene face to Corinne's, now turning red. He
sounded more incredulous than he intended, but, dammit,
why did it seem like he was always in the dark where his
daughter was concerned? "What's this all about?''

When, after a moment of silence, it became apparent
that Corinne wasn't going to speak, Hally jumped into the
breach. "According to Mother, your daughter has quite a
flair for art.''

"Well, I'll be.'' With a pang, Mike recalled that years
ago in college he'd discovered a similar flair in himself.
He'd even flirted with the idea of spending a year in Europe, studying the old masters, soaking up art, culture and
inspiration in such places as Florence and Vienna and the
Left Bank of the Seine.

Reality—his love for Rebecca and the need to get a
degree that would earn him a living so that they could
marry—had steered him on a more practical course, however. Maybe that's why he found himself feeling quite
pleased with the prospect that in his daughter that particular fantasy of his might find fulfillment.

He kept his eyes on Corinne, who flushed more deeply
at Hally's words. He hoped she would look up so he could
show her that he was glad. But she didn't.

Except when he said, "I had no idea...''

"I wonder why,'' she drawled with heavy sarcasm and
a scathing glance.

Mike held on to his temper. Barely. He took a deep
breath and addressed Edith. "Could I see something she's
done?''

Edith's quick "Certainly,'' coincided with Corinne's appalled "No...'' It earned her a look of reproof from the
older woman.

"Rule number one,'' she instructed as she firmly tugged

the girl along. "If you want something from someone you also have to give in return...."

As they ducked into the studio, Mike turned to Hally with a shake of the head and a sigh. "I don't know," he said.

Hally knew it was a general admission of helplessness rather than a comment apropos anything specific. "Give it a chance," she soothed. "And take my word for it, she's not so much belligerent as quaking in those ridiculous shoes of hers. Talking about her art, showing you her sketches, makes her feel vulnerable. As in, what if you don't think they're any good?"

"Hell, I don't care if they're the scribblings of a baboon," Mike countered, exasperated. "If drawing'll make her happy..."

"But that's just it," Hally interrupted in an urgent tone. "She needs more from you than tolerance for a new hobby, she needs your approval, your encouragement, your genuine *recognition* of her very real talent..."

"And she's got it." Mike knew Hally was right in what she was saying. He knew because he remembered only too well the mixture of pride and trepidation he'd felt the one and only time he'd let his own father get a look at some of his work. His best work, work that had earned him lavish praise from his instructor.

Work at which his father—and Rebecca, too, Mike now recalled—had stared with consternation. "What the hell is it?" his father had asked before adding in a kindly, patronizing tone, "Best stick with geology, son...."

Garnet Bloomfield ran Hally to ground some four weeks after Mike Parker and his problems had first walked into Hally's life. September had waned, but so far October had not yet come through with a much welcomed cooling trend. Daytime temperatures continued to hover near ninety.

The two women sat on the terrace of the Blue Lagoon Diner, shaded by a huge umbrella and fanned by a desultory breeze off the water.

"You've been busy," Garnet commented. She sat stiff as a poker and kept her eyes fixed on some distant point offshore.

Watching her, saying nothing, Hally sipped at her white wine spritzer and thought, Uh-oh, she's ticked.

"I called you I don't know how many times," Garnet continued in an injured tone. "At the very least you could've called me back."

"I did." Hally was pretty sure she had, but she'd been so busy.... "I left messages, didn't I?"

"Twice. In three weeks!" Garnet's eyes snapped to Hally's. "And both times you said you'd call me back later and never did."

"I'm sorry." Hally set her glass down, genuinely contrite. "I've had an awful lot on my mind lately."

"Don't tell me." Garnet sniffed. "Let me guess. It's a man."

"It is not." Contrition gave way to a flare of annoyance, especially since she could feel heat rushing into her face. "Why is that always the first thing anyone thinks of? As if there can be no complications in life that don't involve the opposite sex."

"Because more often than not they *are* involved." Garnet tested her frozen margarita and puckered her lips at its tartness. "Besides which, I ran into Gilbert Smith."

She slanted Hally a glance. "He says you dumped him."

"*Dumped* him?" Hally repeated, incredulous.

Garnet shrugged. "My word, not his, but even so." She stabbed at her slushy drink with her straw, all the while eyeing Hally speculatively from beneath half-lowered lashes. "He says there's another man."

"Oh, he does, does he?" Indignation at having been

gossiped about in this fashion made Hally ball her hands into fists with which she would dearly have loved to sock Gilbert Smith in the nose.

"Father of one of your students, he says." Garnet flung down the straw like a gauntlet and her eyes drilled into Hally's. "Well?"

"Gilbert Smith is full of—"

"No argument there," Garnet cut in with a grin. "You'll recall I never did like the man. So cut to the chase."

"There is no chase." And there wasn't, Hally told herself staunchly, but avoided meeting her friend's all-too-seeing eyes by taking at turn at staring out over the water. She'd never been very good at fooling Garnet whom she had known since grade school. And while it was true that there was nothing "going on" between Mike Parker and herself, it was also true that she caught herself wishing there could be more often than she had any business doing.

The irony was that whenever she got near Mike and caught those same vibrations from him, she panicked. And wanted nothing so much as to run in the opposite direction like the scared little rabbit she was.

Once burned....

"Oh, hell." Hally put a hand over her eyes and shook her head at her own folly. Here she hadn't thought of Greg Stahl in years and suddenly...

"What?"

The note of concern in Garnet's voice made Hally drop her hand to look resignedly at her friend. "Remember Greg?"

"From back in college? The jerk you got engaged to? The *louse?*" Garnet looked aghast. "Don't tell me *he's* the guy—"

"Good grief, no!" Hally was appalled her friend would think so for even an instant. "I may be stupid where men are concerned but not *that* stupid."

"Then what?"

"I don't know." Hally toyed with her glass. She was tempted to confide in Garnet, but at the same time reluctant to put into words the conflicting emotions she'd been struggling with. Giving voice to her feelings would be like giving them substance, making them real. But without making them any more acceptable, or possible.

"You're unhappy," Garnet said softly, being strictly a friend now, the way she'd always been. And as Hally had always been to her. They'd shared many a confidence over the years and knew each other well. Too well to be able to keep any secrets.

Which was really the reason Hally had been so negligent about returning her friend's calls. And why she didn't try any longer to prevaricate.

"Confused would be a better word," she admitted with a sigh. "Confused and irritated."

"Irritated? With who?"

"Whom," Hally automatically corrected in her English teacher mode. "Myself." She sipped her wine, warmed it in her mouth before swallowing, and showed Garnet a tiny space between thumb and forefinger. "I'm this close to making the second worst mistake in my life."

"The first being?"

"Falling in love with Gregory Stahl, letting him move in with me, paying the bills for three years while he studied. *Studied.* Ha!" She sliced Garnet a look of disgust about her own gullibility and was, as always, warmed by her friend's commiserating expression. "Boy, was I naive."

"We all were," Garnet said. "But you were vulnerable, too. All that business with your dad…"

"Right." Painful business then, unfinished business now. She hadn't yet worked up the courage to have that adult-level chat with Edith.

Back then, ten years ago, her father had been the enemy.

The villain in the family drama that had devastated her mother and her. She'd only wanted to get away from him, and from what she'd considered his cruel betrayal, as completely as possible. And so she'd been no contest when Greg Stahl, only four years older than her own twenty-two, but decades more sophisticated, had decided it suited his plans to make her fall in love with him.

Greg was everything she'd always longed for James McKenzie to be—kind, loving, attentive. And always there.

She would have done anything for him, and did. Until the day she'd walked in on him making love to another woman in their apartment, in *her* bed. And he hadn't even pretended to be sorry. On the contrary, he'd said it was Hally's own fault for turning into a drudge.

A drudge! Working part-time, studying for her Masters, cooking his meals, doing his laundry... All this she'd done gladly, telling herself it was an investment in their future. Greg's studies were so much more demanding, more important. His Ph.D.... She had even cooked meals for the woman with whom he was cheating on her. Candace Laroux, his supposed study partner. Oh, brother....

She'd kicked him out on his ear, tossed all of his things out of the window in a rage of anger and hurt. And she had promised herself never to trust again, never to let a man past her defenses again.

But lately, for the first time, she wondered if making such a vow might not have been overkill. Things were never just black-and-white. Though she'd always known that intellectually, it was through her dealings with Mike and Corinne that this truism had finally sunk in. And so, maybe her father really wasn't quite the villain she'd pegged him to be. And Greg?

"He married Candy Laroux the minute he got his degree," she told Garnet pensively. "Did you know that?"

"Yes, and they deserve each other," Garnet said, so

righteously on Hally's behalf that Hally couldn't help but laugh.

Though a little sheepishly. "In retrospect, I wonder if I was ever really in love with him."

Certainly the feelings she'd had for him had never been as intensely unsettling as the feelings Mike Parker could arouse with just a glance.

"I, for one, always wondered how you could be," Garnet confessed. "He was such a jerk. He treated you like a doormat."

"I acted like a doormat. I tried to be everything I thought he'd want me to be, say what I thought he wanted to hear. I was afraid I'd lose him if I voiced an opinion of my own."

"I know." Garnet's expression was one of remembered disgust. "I used to want to grab you and shake you till your teeth rattled."

"I wouldn't have thanked you for it."

"I know." Garnet raised her hand to the waiter, signaling for another round of drinks. "Any more than you'd thank me now if I told you to go ahead and make that second worst mistake you mentioned earlier."

October twenty-sixth marked Corinne's fifteenth birthday. It fell on a Saturday. An afternoon at the beach, complete with a picnic supplied by Hally, was planned. Corinne surprised her father by showing up at breakfast dressed in shorts and a top that bared her shoulders and didn't quite reach her waist, but still managed to look demure enough to please Mike.

Two nights ago Corinne had made the final payback of the money she had "borrowed" from the cookie jar cat. She had earned it by cleaning Edith's studio and washing her car every week in addition to baby-sitting Warlock Swigert every Monday after school. She was also getting paid now for doing chores at home.

And even though she gave him the money with no more than her usual desultory style, Mike was encouraged. Corinne was toeing the line, she was living up to the terms of her parole, and she looked a heck of a lot more like the kind of young girl Mike considered "proper."

He owed it all to Halloran. The woman was subtly but inexorably becoming a major presence in their lives. A friend to his daughter. But *what* to him?

It was a question that lately had been robbing him of sleep. Right along with, What did he *want* her to be to him?

He had already admitted his attraction to her. And she had admitted feeling likewise drawn to him. Only to turn around and tell him, "Hands off. Not interested. Not smart. Not possible." A lot of "nots."

"Don't look. Don't touch. Don't want." A lot of "don'ts." And they were starting to really tick him off. The longer he knew Halloran McKenzie, the better he got to know her, the more he liked who she was.

And, of course, that womanly shape of hers had lit his fire right from the start. He wanted her. Craved her. *Needed* her. So maybe it was time to make her see that she needed him, too.

He was sure that Corinne would understand if he and Halloran were to get...closer. She liked Halloran. She adored Edith. It made sense that she'd like and adore them even more if they became an even bigger part of their lives. Didn't it?

So what was he thinking? *Marriage?* Mike gulped; sweat broke out. The very word made his stomach drop into his shoes. So okay, if not marriage, what? A flaming affair?

He mentally rolled his eyes—yeah, sure. Because even if Hally were inclined to go along with something like that—in a pig's eye!—what kind of role models would that make them for Corinne?

So what *was* he thinking?

"I'm thinking you're getting way ahead of yourself here, bud."

Funny how saying something out loud could make a guy see sense. *You don't start running, you walk awhile first.* In man-woman terms that meant you *dated* awhile before considering anything beyond...well, friendship. You maybe took in a movie together. Or you had a nice dinner out. Stuff like that. Yup. Right. Ask her out, that's what he'd do.

And she'd say no.

Okay. Fine. Being prepared for that, he'd then simply have to find a way to change her mind.

The question was how? How to make Halloran Mc-Kenzie recant her Hands Off edict. How could he make her like him, want him, *love* him enough to trust him and give him a shot?

Because *trust*—the lack of, the betrayal of—was what it came down to with her. Of that Mike had no doubt. They'd talked enough and confided enough of their private lives to each other in the course of their close association these past seven weeks for him to know that she'd been hurt.

Seven weeks. In many ways a very short time. In others, a lifetime. He felt like he'd known Halloran McKenzie forever. It seemed like forever since he'd walked into her office. Forever since he'd argued with her, fought with her about how to "rescue" Corinne.

A month, he'd said, that's all he'd give her. Well, the month had stretched into seven weeks without a murmur from him....

Hally didn't care to remember that she had meant her private sessions with Corinne to be a temporary, short-term arrangement. She had purchased an Italian language course on tape, listening to it as she commuted to and from school so that her evenings could be free.

She had invested in a stationary bicycle and worked out on it for forty minutes every other morning before school. She told herself it was simply easier than trying to make it to those aerobics classes. And, hey, her efforts were paying off.

As recently as last August the white clamdiggers she was wearing for Corinne's birthday picnic had been uncomfortably snug around the hips. While today...

"Great suit," Mike commented with an appreciative sweep of Hally's lush curves after she'd slipped off her abbreviated ducks and cotton shirt to reveal a sleek black maillot.

"Thanks." Hally busied herself with folding her clothes and tucking them into the oversize beach bag. She knew she would blush if she'd let her eyes meet the masculine ones she could still feel on her body like a lover's touch. "Corinne's the one who chose it, actually. During our shopping spree the other day."

"In that case I'm doubly impressed," Mike said, though in fact he was more than merely impressed by the sight of this woman. He was enthralled because stripped down to near nothing, Halloran McKenzie was all of his fantasies come to breathtaking life.

And more. Much more. She stirred his soul as well as his blood, and she made him think of the future in terms that, not too long ago, would have had him running in the opposite direction. She was a woman he now desperately longed to pull into his arms and kiss into breathless delirium.

Forced to be civilized in this public place, he surged to his feet and grabbed Hally's hand. "Come on, let's go for a swim."

"We can't." Hally dug in her heels, but gloried in the

feel of her hand in Mike's. "Corinne'll be right back with those sodas."

"Somehow I doubt it." Mike pointed to where, not fifteen feet away, his still-empty-handed daughter stood talking—and laughing—with a deeply tanned, handsome young man. Mike frowned as his fatherly antenna went up. "Isn't that the kid who cuts your grass? Joey something-or-other?"

"Joey Gonzales?" Hally squinted against the sun. "Yes, it is. What? Oh, she's bringing him over."

Snatching her hand out of Mike's, flustered, she bent to retrieve her sunglasses. She put them on her nose and felt much better able to cope with the devastating proximity of Mike Parker's muscular body in abbreviated trunks. The thatch of graying chest hair that trailed, funnel-shaped, past his trim midriff and beyond made her fingers itch for a touch.

"Hi," she called brightly as the two young people drew near. They made an eye-catching couple—Joey's Latin swarthiness the perfect foil for Corinne's alabaster fairness. With her hair grown into face-framing softness and dyed a startling but surprisingly becoming shade of magenta, Corinne's large eyes and delicate facial structure came into their own. She was a very pretty young woman.

With a pang, Mike was taking note of that, too. But he also took note of the way the boy, Joey, was ogling his daughter, and felt another stab of emotion that was much less poignant and benign, and much more aggressive. It made his hands curl into fists, and the order, "Keep your eyes to yourself, boy," leaped to his tongue.

Fortunately, some shred of sanity made him swallow the words and drag a carefully neutral expression up out of somewhere. He replied with a mute nod to Joey's slightly uncertain greeting.

"I was wondering if Corinne could come and play volleyball?'' Joey flicked a glance, as though for support, to Hally as he asked.

She glanced at Mike whose immediate reaction was to say no. But he was uncomfortably aware of the three pairs of eyes that were trained on him with a variety of expressions. Though only two of those pairs truly mattered—Hally's and Corinne's.

''It's Cory's birthday,'' he replied evasively. ''We're here for a picnic.''

''I thought maybe Joey could share it with us later,'' Corinne stunned Mike by interjecting. It was the first time she had voluntarily addressed him in a nonconfrontational manner. ''We've got plenty of food now that Edith didn't come.''

She turned pleading eyes to Hally. ''Don't we, Ms. McKenzie?''

''Well, I... Sure, but...'' Hally glanced at Mike's shuttered face. She wished Corinne hadn't drawn her into this. She didn't relish being put in a position to choose sides. ''It's up to your father...''

''Please, Dad.'' It was the tone—softly entreating—as much as the hesitantly hopeful expression on Cory's face that annihilated the last of Michael's resistance.

''Why not?'' he muttered. ''Go ahead. Have fun.'' The gruffness in his voice was his poor attempt to cover up his welling emotions.

He lost the battle completely, however, when with a jubilant, ''Thanks, Dad,'' Corinne blew him a kiss as she dashed off with Joey.

He turned away to hide the moisture blinding his eyes. His fists opened and closed and he took deep breaths. He wished he could... If only there was...

He didn't know what exactly it was he needed just then until Hally stepped in front of him and opened her arms.

He stepped into them blindly and she held him. Just held him while he struggled to come to grips with his emotions.

There was nothing sexual in their embrace though Mike had buried his face in the fragrant warmth of Hally's neck and their bodies touched. Neither wanted anything of the other but to give comfort and to take it.

And neither could have pinpointed that instant in time when it changed.

When awareness replaced the sense of nurturing friendship. When excitement replaced the glow of affection. And when carnal desire replaced the desire to soothe and be soothed.

Just like that, it was there. The tightening of a muscle, a sharply drawn breath. It drew them apart, slowly, hesitantly, as if they were afraid of what they'd see when they were face-to-face.

They stared into each other's eyes, Mike reaching out and taking the sunglasses off Hally's nose. He tossed them down on their blanket without taking his eyes from hers. He was stunned by their expression—hunger, need, a wistful kind of longing.

All the things he was feeling. Except he felt one more—gratitude.

And as he watched the shutters fall over Hally's eyes, blanking out the emotions he thought he had seen, Mike tamped down his own wayward feelings by focusing on that gratitude and nothing else.

"Thank you," he said, managing a crooked smile of self-deprecation at the weakness he'd been helpless to prevent Hally from witnessing. "Sorry about that. She caught me off guard. I'd about given up hope."

He stepped away, and when Hally offered no resistance, consoled himself with the reminder that he had time. And that a public beach park was, in any case, hardly the place for physically reacting to the emotions he had seen in Hally McKenzie's eyes, whether she was prepared to admit to them or not.

Hally was not. Or, at least, she was not ready to admit

them to Mike. It was devastating enough to admit them to herself. Talk about inappropriate. Talk about shameful, to let carnal thoughts and urges intrude on what had been such a deeply emotional moment for Mike.

"I want you to know I give you all the credit," he was saying. He was composed again, rubbing sunscreen over his arms and chest.

Watching him, Hally's throat went dry and she ached to take over the chore. To offer to do his back...

"You and your mother," Mike said. His thoughts paralleled hers in that he was presently flirting with the idea of offering to do Hally's back. He decided that after the awkwardness of moments ago, he'd best keep things light and his hands to himself. "I don't know where Cory and I would be without the two of you."

"Don't forget Joey." Hally uncapped her own suntan lotion for lack of anything better with which to occupy her hands. She tried to relax, to simulate Mike's unselfconscious attitude. It proved, she reminded herself, that she'd been completely off base in thinking he'd desired her, too, those few moments ago in her arms. And that she'd come awfully close to making a fool of herself before she'd come to her senses. "In this case I think it's he, and true love, rather than Mom and me who—"

"True lo-ve?" Shock made Mike draw the word into two syllables. "My God, she's only a baby."

"She's fifteen," Hally reminded him, glad to have something else to focus on besides Michael Parker's impressive physique. "How old were you when you had your first crush?" She burst into laughter at the look on his face. "I bet you're thinking that was different, right?"

"You a mind reader now?"

"No." Hally adjusted the beach umbrella she'd brought to partially shade them and their ice chest full of food. "It's a parent's standard response, that's all." She slanted him glance of teasing challenge. "So how old were you?"

"Thirteen," Mike admitted. He tossed the tube of sunscreen aside and stretched out on his back. "How about you?"

"I was a late bloomer." Hally sat back, folding her legs in the lotus position and recalling the terrible crush she'd had on the biggest jock of her senior class, football ace Chuck Alberton. "I was seventeen. And he never even knew I existed."

"Just goes to show," Mike muttered with an air of languor that was all pretense because admiring Hally's nubile form from below half-lowered eyelids had him anything but relaxed.

"Goes to show what?" Hally, too, was doing her share of looking and longing in between picking at tufts of grass.

"That most teenage boys are morons."

That made her laugh. "And those who aren't?"

"Are the ones you oughta watch out for. Which reminds me…" Mike abruptly sat up and got to his feet. "Come on." He held out his hand to help her up.

Still too nervous about touching him to accept his assistance, Hally pretended not to see his hand as she rose by herself. "Where're we going?"

"To watch a volleyball game, where else?"

As it turned out, they weren't allowed to be mere spectators for long. They were drafted to play on opposing teams and, to Corinne's undisguised surprise and not quite so obvious pride, Mike distinguished himself as the star of their team.

Hally's team was soundly trounced, a victory they were well on their way to overturning, however, during the game of water polo that followed.

Hally, California Coast born and raised, was no stranger to water sports and an excellent player. Mike was spiking a shot in her direction when, with a frisson of alarm that raised goose bumps, he realized that she was in trouble out there toward the deep.

She was visibly struggling to keep her head above water. Her face was contorted, her eyes wide and panicked. Her arms were thrashing around.

Mike absorbed all this in a flash. He launched himself toward her, unaware that Corinne was doing the same. And just as Hally went under.

Afterward, for Hally, the rescue was all pretty much a blur. But she remembered the sudden, excruciating cramp in her calf that had struck out of nowhere. She'd been treading water, arms up in anticipation of the killer shot she could see Mike was getting ready to fire her way. She remembered thinking, with malicious glee, that the opposition's desperation was showing.

And then the pain had struck. She remembered doubling over—a reaction as reflexive as the gasp of distress that made her open her mouth that, in turn, had caused her to swallow what seemed like gallons of briny seawater.

Choking and spluttering, she couldn't draw breath to cry out. And she couldn't seem to keep herself afloat or grab hold of anyone or anything, no matter how desperately she swung her arms.

She remembered her eyes connecting with Mike's the second time she surfaced. How shock and comprehension had widened his. And how she had prayed and tried to call out to him....

Going under that third time had been almost a relief. Her right leg was rigid with cramp but she barely felt the pain now at all. She was tiring.

But not yet so tired she didn't latch on with desperate strength to the slim streak of purple that had shot past her and grabbed her up. Corinne...

Hally didn't know that's who it had been until quite some time later when she'd been purged of seawater, wrapped in a blanket and given a clean bill of health by the lifeguard who'd belatedly rounded out Hally's trio of heroes.

Corinne and Mike deserved the brunt of the glory. Corinne, who'd been a member of her school swim team in Idaho, had reached her only split seconds before Mike. Together they had maneuvered Hally to shore where Mike had immediately worked on her. The by-then-alerted lifeguard had arrived in time to watch Hally violently expel the ingested salt water amid mortified mutterings of, "I'm sorry," as though she were committing some breach of etiquette.

She was adamant in her refusal to be taken home. "I'm fine," she said staunchly, and she was, too. Especially after the massage Mike had given her leg; it had warmed and limbered up her calf muscle. And quite a few other places, as well. Not that she was about to let him know that. She said, "I wouldn't necessarily want to eat anything, having just swallowed and spit out half of the Pacific, but other than that, I just need to catch my breath."

Mike had secured a lounge for her and, semisomnolent, she lolled in it now and took pleasure in watching her picnic being devoured by half a dozen young people, all of whom seemed to think Corinne Parker was pretty okay.

Hally certainly thought so. And as she risked a glance at Mike, who had wrapped himself in a silence she was hesitant to intrude upon as he watched his daughter interact with her new friends, she hoped that that was what he was thinking, too.

She shifted her gaze and caught Corinne's eyes. They glowed with an inner light that had never been there before. Happiness. Pride. Self-confidence.

Closing her own, Hally thought that if nearly drowning had helped put that light there, then it had certainly been worth it.

On the way home, Mike reflected somewhat wryly that he and his daughter seemed to always find themselves in a car in the immediate wake of some momentous occasion.

Rebecca's funeral. That godawful concert mess. The court hearing, and now this.

The marked difference was—this had started and ended as a happy occasion. Corinne's party had been a success, and the woman he had come to...care for was alive and well. Thanks to his daughter's quick thinking.

"That was a wonderful thing you did." He changed lanes, slanting Corinne a quick smile between glances in the rearview and side mirrors.

One of them briefly connected with a frowning look from her. "You already said that. Twice." She looked away. "And anyway, you did more than I did."

Given her somewhat martyred tone, Mike decided to let the topic rest. He took a corner a little too fast and made himself take a deep breath. He wondered if Corinne was miffed because she'd wanted to ride home in Joey's car but Mike had said no. The way he saw it, one entire afternoon in the company of a boy he'd had no idea his child had been interested in was long enough. Besides, he wasn't at all sure he was ready to deal with this boy-girl business, no matter what Hally said.

He'd been braced for Corinne's snarled objection when he'd insisted she ride home with him. But she had once more succeeded in surprising him by doing the unexpected. With Joey and Hally looking on, she'd complied with a docile nod of acceptance. Too docile?

Mike took another deep breath. "Want to listen to some music?"

"No, thank you."

Well, at least she'd said thank you. Mike turned on the radio anyway. An Oldies station. Good gravy, Elvis singing about blue suede shoes....

That was old, even for him. He'd grown up with the Beatles, Bread and the Jackson Five. He fleetingly wondered whatever had become of Alice Cooper. And which groups Halloran McKenzie might have been partial to.

Halloran... He heaved a sigh, glanced at his daughter, and wished life weren't so damned complicated. If he'd had his druthers, he'd be with Halloran now. They had dropped her off at her house. He'd seen her in, but she'd insisted she didn't need him and Cory to hang around till Edith came home from her day with Bill O'Rourke.

"I'm fine," she had assured him, same as she had all along. "I would have let you take me home long before this if I weren't."

"You look wiped." Mike had hated leaving her, even knowing she was taking herself straight to bed. Which was exactly the place he was just dying to take her. Not that he'd let her know that.

He'd said, "I know darned good and well you only stayed so Cory's picnic party wouldn't be dampened by what happened."

"What happened is that I owe you and that amazing kid of yours a whole lot of thanks."

He'd waved off the thanks, but as to the other... "She *is* pretty amazing, isn't she?"

He thought so now, and sliced her another glance. She sat so primly, hands folded in her lap, eyes focused straight ahead. Her hair—Lord, what a color!—was slicked back now after all that swimming and the style somehow highlighted the delicacy of her face in profile. A face, so it seemed to him, that only weeks ago had still been softly rounded by baby fat.

His little girl was growing up. Soon she would go off on her own. Leave him behind. *His* little girl.

Mike smothered a humorless chuckle. The sad truth was, she had never been his. And it hurt like hell to admit that. But it hurt even more to think that all too soon he would lose her for good...without having been in her heart.

He wanted to tell her how proud he was of her. Her lightning-quick reflexes, her cool head and swift action had saved a woman's life. He took a deep breath. Struggled for the words. Words that, with anyone else, would have come to his tongue with ease and enthusiasm.

Why was it always so damned hard for him to say to the people who mattered to him most the words that were in his heart? Why couldn't he simply let his feelings guide his tongue as other people seemed able to do?

So what if Corinne tossed his words back at him? So what if she turned her head and rebuffed his every attempt to establish rapport? If he tried often enough, said the right things repeatedly enough, one fine day they were bound to be heard and accepted.

Or so Halloran McKenzie had assured him.

Mike stole another glance at his daughter. Her head was bowed now. She looked...sad. Dejected...

"Cory?" He reached out, tentatively. He touched her hair. "You okay?"

A quick shake of the head. A stifled snuffle. Mike's heart twisted. Dear Lord, she was crying. What should he do?

His ingrained male helplessness in the face of female tears was exacerbated by a crushing sense of guilt and feelings of inadequacy. What kind of father was he, to cause his only child to cry on her birthday?

"What's the matter, honey?" He awkwardly patted her shoulder and pulled back his hand when she stiffened. "I'm here if you want to talk about it."

Cory sniffled and shrugged. "I guess I miss Mom," she said in a tear-clogged voice. "Being my birthday and all...."

"Mom would've been so darned proud of you," Mike said, unable to come up with anything else to comfort her. "*I'm* proud of you. What you did today was pretty incredible. I had no idea you could swim like that."

"That's because you don't know me." The tear-streaked face she turned to him near broke Mike's heart, as did her words. "Don't you see? You never took the time to get to know me."

She didn't yell. She didn't snarl. She spoke quietly, tearfully, regretfully. Mike would almost have preferred the contempt to this poignant sadness.

Apologies rushed to his tongue. Explanations, rationalizations. But then he thought, Wait a minute!

And he said, "It wasn't by choice I was gone so much. It was necessity. I was away making a living, Corinne. And I think you're old enough now to understand that."

"And when you were home?"

"When I was home you retreated from me like a stranger."

"Because you *were* a stranger," she cried, twisting around to glare at him with streaming eyes. "You'd come into the house and everything would change. Mom changed. She'd get all grouchy and wouldn't be fun anymore. She wouldn't have time for me. When you were away she'd always do things with me when I couldn't see my friends. She was mine. We were best friends. She always said so. Except—"

"Except when I was around," Mike finished quietly when Corinne, with a choked sob, turned to stare out the window. "Seems to me, little girl, that the trouble isn't that I didn't want you, but that you didn't want me."

And that your mother did nothing to change that, he thought bitterly. *Quite the contrary...*

Corinne didn't react to his words. As soon as he pulled up at the curb, she struggled to open the door.

Mike restrained her by placing a gentle hand on her shoulder. She stiffened again, but this time he didn't let go. "Like it or not," he said quietly, "Mom is gone and I am all you've got. You're all I've got."

He cupped her chin and urged her face around. He put his face close to hers, but she refused to meet his eyes. He said, "Don't you think it's time you gave this thing a chance?"

She didn't answer. She wouldn't look at him. But she no longer struggled to get away, either. Mike took heart from that and stayed as he was. Waiting. Hoping. Praying. Because he'd given it his best shot and he didn't know what else he could say, unless it was...

"I love you, baby." The words came of their own volition. And when, with a sob, Corinne buried her face against his chest, the words came again. His arms closed around her and he held his child against his heart.

Chapter Eight

It was a start. A turning point. Mike hadn't expected a miraculous change to take place and that was just as well because he would have been disappointed.

In the days that followed, the best that could be said was that tensions had eased. Corinne cooperated, she did her chores, applied herself at school and at Edith's, and was even cordial to him. Sometimes.

"She's a teenager," Hally explained with some amusement when Mike grumbled about the unpredictability of his daughter's moods. "Unpredictability, surliness on the heels of utter sweetness—these are a teen's stock in trade. Best to accept whatever comes your way with equanimity."

"She's never moody around whatshisname."

"Joey," Hally supplied, adding, "Of course not. Him, she wants to impress."

"Humph." Mike frowned at the crowd of students pouring out of the school. A surprising number of them were couples. High school sweethearts... He sighed. That's what he and Rebecca had been, too, in their day. Crazy in love and certain the future belonged to them. And for a while there it had....

"What's keeping that girl?" he grumbled, glancing at his watch, more to show Hally he was as anxious to be getting home—he wasn't—as she probably was.

Actually Hally wasn't anxious, either. They had met by chance on the school steps—or, at least, that would have been Hally's story if anyone had asked. No way would she have admitted—she barely admitted it to herself—that on Mondays, Wednesdays and Fridays she dropped everything at the ring of the bell and charged out of the building like a Thoroughbred out of a starting gate just to catch a glimpse of Mike before he and Corinne drove off.

They didn't see much of each other otherwise. Tuesdays and Thursdays she gave Corinne a ride from school to Edith's, and Joey invariably showed up to drive her home. The two Saturdays since the birthday picnic, Mike had simply dropped his daughter at the curb in front of the duplex and, again, Joey had driven her home.

Mike was avoiding her. Hally knew it, was miserable over it, but didn't have the nerve to come right out and say something. What could she say without sounding needy? "Hey, I've changed my mind. I think I would like us to be...friends, after all?" No way. Besides, it wasn't "friends" she wanted to be with him, was it?

And what she did want to be with him was still just as impossible as she'd told him it was that day in her yard. Wasn't it?

She still didn't want to put her heart at risk again for a man. She still had her goals, her plans to travel, to take that Italian sabbatical.

Yet if that was true, then why didn't she go to her Italian language class now that she had the time? Why didn't she even listen anymore to those language tapes she had bought?

And why did she run and skulk and breathlessly hang

around simply to catch a glimpse of this man who seemed to have completely forgotten that he'd once been attracted to her? Why did she dream of him at night and wish he were with her by day? Why, when he spoke to her, would she stare at his lips and wonder how they'd feel pressed to hers? When he spoke to her—

"Uh...what?" With a start, Hally snapped her eyes up to Mike's as she realized he was speaking to her. And that he was gazing at her with a most peculiar expression.

"Where'd you go?" he asked, his voice husky. "The look on your face made me want to follow you there."

Oh, God. Hally's face flamed and she uttered a small sound of mortification. "I'm sorry," she mumbled, averting her face.

Mike wouldn't let her. He caught her chin. "Don't be," he said, holding her eyes and letting her see the emotions she'd evoked in him even as he forced a teasing note into his voice. "Not if you were thinking of me."

"Maybe I was." Good grief, had she actually said that?

Mike's burning gaze told her she had. "Then maybe it's time we had a talk," he said. "A serious talk. In private. What do you say?"

For a moment Hally could say nothing. She swallowed, her eyes clinging to his. She nervously licked her lips and wondered if she dare take the plunge. And just when she was ready to, it was too late.

"Corinne," Mike said, his gaze shifting beyond Hally as he removed his hand from her chin. The ardent expression of seconds ago might never have been there, so thoroughly had he erased it.

Hally, turning slowly to watch the girl approach, could have wept. She released a long breath that was, to her chagrin, audibly shaky.

Mike's quick glance made it clear he had heard. He seemed pleased. Hally's heart skipped a beat.

"Hi, Ms. McKenzie." Corinne was alone. And surprisingly eager, because after a perfunctory, "Hi, Dad," she breathlessly added, "So, have you talked to her?"

What was this? Hally turned questioning eyes to Mike. His expression was enigmatic and he held Hally's gaze as he told his daughter, "We talked, but not about that."

"About what?" Hally, mystified and fearful of what Corinne might read into a prolonged eye contact, shifted her gaze to her student.

Corinne, in turn, looked accusingly at her father. "But you promised."

"And I meant it. Here." He handed her the keys to his car. "Go on ahead to the car while I walk Ms. McKenzie to hers and talk to her now."

Corinne took the keys, but, poised to go, looked at Hally with a puzzling mixture of entreaty and hope. "See ya," she said in a tentative voice. Then quickly walked away.

Hally frowned up at Mike as she walked beside him down the steps. "What was that all about?"

"A date."

"A *date?*" Hally's heart flipped. Could it be Corinne wanted to play matchmaker between her father and...

"Joey wants to take Cory to the movies." Mike unwittingly dashed Hally's half-hopeful assumption, making her feel foolish. And glad he couldn't read minds. "Tonight."

"I see." But since she really didn't, she asked, "So where do I come in?"

"Well..." Mike let Hally precede him through the narrow space between cars in the teacher's lot. "Corinne suggested that since I was—to put it mildly—less than enthusiastic about the idea, I should discuss it with you, whom she obviously considers more than passing cool, or whatever the term is these days.

"An opinion I share, by the way," he unsettled Hally anew by adding.

"Why, thank you, kind sir." She fumbled with the key in the car door to hide her blush. Straightening after unlocking the door, she found herself practically chin-to-chest with Mike who loomed over her with one hand on the roof of her VW and one on the adjacent, rusting Subaru.

With a nervous little laugh, she glanced around at the busy lot and retreated a step. "So are you asking me if Corinne should be allowed to go?"

"In essence, yes." Mike was inordinately pleased and encouraged by Hally's flustered reaction to him. He had resigned himself to staying away from her and it had been sheer torture. Now, it seemed, things were looking up. "I also wondered just how trustworthy this Gonzales kid really is."

"Well, for starters, 'this Gonzales kid's' name is Joey." Hally wasn't sure where the flare of annoyance had come from. Yes, she was—Mike's intonation. "As to trustworthy, let's see. He's the oldest of four, his mother is widowed, he works two jobs and is an honor student, a senior, across town at Garibaldi High. Besides tending our lawns, he regularly house-sits for my mother and me, and Chaucer thinks he's the best thing since catnip."

She thrust out her chin and glared at Mike whose eyebrows had all but disappeared into his hairline. "Trustworthy enough for you, Mr. Parker?"

"Yes, ma'am." Mike stifled a chuckle and resisted the urge to reach out and smooth the frown off her forehead. "I obviously pushed some kind of button."

"You did." Not yet relenting because there was amusement in his eyes, Hally sternly held his gaze. "I have no patience with bigotry, no matter how benign."

"And you think I'm a bigot for caring about my daughter's welfare?" It surprised Mike how much it stung to have her misjudge him like this. "I'd be a poor excuse of a father if I didn't."

"Of course you would. And I didn't mean that." Taking

a deep breath, Hally admitted to herself that she might have overreacted. "It's the way you said his name."

Mike frowned at her, at a loss.

"Sort of...deprecatingly," Hally elaborated with an embarrassed little laugh. She had overreacted. "I guess I'm a little overprotective where Joey's concerned. He tries so hard, but just because he's a little rough around the edges and he's got a Latino name, some people tend to..."

She faltered beneath Mike's hard stare.

"And you think I'm one of those people?" he asked, more insulted than he could ever remember being. "I would have thought you'd know me better than that by now."

He pushed past her and stalked away.

"Mike!" Hally spun around and glared after him. "Darn it!"

"Lover's quarrel?"

Gilbert Smith. Hally closed her eyes and silently counted to ten before turning to where he lounged against his battered Subaru with a supercilious smirk on his face. She wondered how she could ever have found him appealing.

She opened her mouth for a snappy rejoinder, but closed it again when nothing came to mind that wouldn't make her sound petty and snide. Tossing her head, she dismissed him with a glance and got into her car.

When Hally pulled into her driveway, Edith was on her own side of the house, fondly kissing Bill O'Rourke goodbye. Still out of sorts with herself, Gilbert Smith, Mike Parker and the world in general, Hally tossed them a brief wave and headed into the house without stopping to chat.

She should have known this would prompt Edith to follow her posthaste, and indignantly. "You were rude to Bill, Halloran."

"I was not." Hally down tossed her keys and put on

the kettle. More to occupy her hands than from a desire
for tea. "I simply didn't want to intrude on your tender
scene."

She leaned against the counter and crossed her arms.
"So. Are you in love with him, Mother?" Her own dis-
satisfactions made her tone almost strident.

And she felt instantly ashamed of it when Edith quietly
asked, "Don't you want me to be?"

"Of course I do, Mom." Hally puffed out a loud breath
and shook her head. "Don't mind me. I don't know what's
the matter..."

"I do," Edith said softly. She came to stand next to
Hally and smoothed back a curl. "I think you're lonely,
sweetheart. I think you're—"

"No." Furious, Hally ducked away from her mother's
hand. "Don't start with me, Mom. Please—"

"Why shouldn't I start?" Though as a rule Hally's for-
bidding tone was enough to silence Edith, today she refused to be hushed. Flushed with agitation, she demanded,
"Why shouldn't I worry when year in, year out I watch
you bury yourself in your work, fretting over other people's children when you should be rearing your own. When
you should be in love, and happily married."

"*Happily* married?" Hally spun around with a bitter
little laugh, one hand on her hip in a challenging stance.
"Mother, you of all people should know that's a contra-
diction in terms."

"No such thing!" Edith exclaimed with an appalled expression on her face. She twisted around as Hally stalked
past her to the stove and snapped the burner off. "Your
father and I had many happy years..."

"Ha!"

"And it was my fault more than his that they came to
an end."

"What!" Hally glared at her mother, then tossed up her

hands in a dramatic gesture of exasperation. "Mother, please. I was there, remember?"

"Yes, I remember. I remember that you were a child."

"A child?" What had gotten into her mother? Hally was shocked and seething. Had she lost her good sense from that bump on the head? "I was fifteen years old. Hardly a child. And I was well past twenty-one when it all hit the fan."

Hally stabbed the air in front of Edith's chest with an accusing finger. "So don't you tell me who was guilty of what around here."

"But I am telling you. And should have done years ago." Edith caught Hally's rigid finger and held on to it. "And you're going to listen because what you think you know is not the truth."

"Oh, really?" Though Hally tried to sound sarcastic, something in her mother's expression—an immense sorrow and regret—made her breath hitch, spoiling the effect. "Like what don't I know?"

"That I had an abortion against your father's express wishes."

"What!" Hally stared at her mother, openmouthed. "But…" She faltered, unable to think of a thing to say. She was flabbergasted, speechless.

Edith released Hally's finger and sank into a chair. She studied her hands, fisted now in her lap. "I lied to him," she said tonelessly. "I promised him I wouldn't do it. He so badly wanted the child…"

"But," Hally said again, then closed her mouth and swallowed bile. She was horrified by what her mother was saying. Not because she was against abortions per se—she believed in free choice. But to do such a thing knowing that your husband…

"You were ill," Hally whispered, gripping her mother's shoulders, her eyes desperately searching for she knew not what in Edith's face. It had become so ghostly pale, the

gash on her forehead stood out like a scarlet brand.
"That's why you did it, Mom. Sure it was. I remember
now. You even had to go to the hospital and—"

"No." Edith laid her hands on top of Hally's when her
daughter would have pulled away. Her eyes, dark with
pain, gazed unflinchingly into Hally's. "All that was afterward. To fix things up. You see, because of your father's
prominence in the medical community here, I had gone to
some…"

"No." The denial was little more than an anguished
moan as Hally gave her mother's shoulders a little shake.
"Oh, Mom. Why?"

"Because I was selfish." Edith bit her lip and, if possible, grew paler still. But she didn't avert her eyes, didn't
try to hide from Hally the extent of her guilt and remorse.
"I wanted my art. I'd had enough of motherhood after
raising Morgan and you almost single-handedly. Your father had his work. You girls were almost done with high
school. I couldn't bear the thought of starting all over again
with a new baby."

Now she did look away, and Hally slowly straightened.
She stared down at her mother's bent head. There was no
gray in Edith's still-luxuriant ash-blond hair. She asked
herself how someone she held so dear and felt so close to
could, at the same time, be a person she didn't know at
all.

"Your father couldn't see that," Edith said. "He had
always wanted another child, but I had somehow managed
to put him off. When I found myself pregnant, I was devastated. He was ecstatic. He was hoping that this time it
would be a boy.

"Not that he didn't love you girls," Edith hastened to
add with a quick glance at Hally, who stifled a dismayed
gasp as it hit her that her disdain for her father might well
have no foundation at all.

Tears she couldn't choke back rose into her eyes. She

felt like covering her ears; she didn't want to hear any more.

But her mother, once having started, seemed determined to make a clean slate. "He vowed that, no matter the baby's gender, he would be more of a hands-on father. And with his practice at last well established, he likely would've been, too. According to your sister, he certainly seems to be completely devoted to... Well, you know."

"His son with Eva," Hally finished in shaky whisper when her mother let the sentence hang. She dropped down onto the chair and with her elbows on the table, cradled her head in her hands. "Does Morgan know? These things you've told me?"

"I don't know. Not from me, though she's so close to your father he might have... I don't know. When, as you put it, 'it all hit the fan,' James left it to me to tell you girls or not..."

"And you chose not to tell." Hally was furious, suddenly. She dropped her hands with a thud. "How dare you? All these years..."

She looked away, unable to bear just then the sight of her mother's devastated face. Taking several deep breaths, she tamped down the urge to scream. "All these years I've been blaming Dad," she said finally, tiredly. "And you let me."

"I know."

"*I know?*" Renewed outrage made Hally's head whip around. "That's all you have to say? *I know?*" Her voice rose. "Mother, you *lied* to me!"

"Only by omission," Edith said in defense of herself, but weakly. "Out of cowardice, out of fear. I'd lost your father and I didn't want to lose my daughters, too. Hally, please..." She held out her hands like a supplicant. "I never spoke badly of your father to you."

"That's right." Hally swung away, livid. "You didn't. You didn't have to. Because by merely maintaining a martyred silence while I jumped to all the wrong conclusions and banished my father from my life you accomplished the same thing.''

Hurt, feeling betrayed beyond bearing, Hally clapped a hand to her mouth as a ragged sob escaped her. "How could you?" she asked brokenly, then snatched up her bag and bolted.

Her mind and emotions in an uproar, her heart broken, Hally drove around aimlessly for a while. Fortunately, this part of town was quiet and the streets at midday almost deserted. As inattentive as she was, she would have been a menace in any kind of traffic.

She felt as if the ground had dropped out from under her and there no longer was a solid foundation for anything in her life. Her life... Her mother...

Hally's mind boggled at the enormity of it all. Her stomach heaved. She pressed a hand to her midsection and pulled the car over to the curb. She killed the engine and let her forehead drop against the steering wheel.

Her father. *There is a lot you don't know, Halloran.*

Oh, dear God. A choked sob escaped her and she bit down hard on her lower lip. She concentrated on breathing. Deeply. Evenly. She rolled down the window to let in a blast of heat. But a bit of a breeze came in, as well. Enough to supply some needed fresh air.

"Halloran?"

Mike had to repeat her name and touch her shoulder before Hally's head came up. She blinked at him, red eyed and looking sick.

"What's wrong?" Alarm sharpened his tone. "Is it Cory?"

"Cory?" Hally repeated, dazed and confused. Where had Mike Parker come from?

Her bewildered reaction made it clear to Mike that his

daughter was not the reason for Halloran McKenzie's distress. The worst of his anxiety abated.

"What's wrong?" he asked again, shaken by how deeply he was affected by this woman's anguish. He had to fight an urge to open the car door and haul her into his arms to protect her and comfort her. "How can I help?"

"Help?" Hally stared up at him, at a loss. "Where'd you come from?" she asked hoarsely. Her throat was raw from the pool of scalding tears she refused to shed. "What're you doing here?"

"I live here." Mike pointed, and Hally's eyes followed to the garish pink house behind him. "You drove here," he said, frowning as he searched her face and saw only bewilderment. "Didn't you know?"

Hally shook her head. "No."

"Come inside. Good thing I came home from the office to change clothes." Thoroughly shaken by Hally's odd demeanor, Mike opened the car door and helped her out.

Dazed, Hally allowed him to lead her inside. To press her down onto the sofa. To sit down beside her and take her ice-cold hands into the warm strength of his.

"I'm sorry," she croaked, her eyes averted while she struggled against the rush of tears scalding her throat. "I shouldn't...be here. You...I mean, I...we're—"

Her voice broke. And when Mike gently urged her face around and said, "You're exactly where you should be," she could hold back the tears no longer.

With a strangled sob, she buried her face against his chest and cried. She cried for herself, for lost years and shattered illusions. And she cried for the father she had never really known.

Mike held her, soothed her, stroked her. And later, when the worst of the deluge was past and Hally, exhausted, nevertheless felt the need to talk, he gave her some space, sat back and listened.

"I'll bet you think it's pretty ironic," she said when

she'd told all and sat twisting into a soggy knot the hand-
kerchief Mike had earlier, wordlessly, put into her hand.
She dabbed at the corner of her eyes, sniffled, and finally
met his gaze. "I mean, that someone as screwed up about
their father as I've been would presume to tell you and
Cory how to run your lives."

Mike hadn't been thinking that and told her so. "The
way I see it," he added, reaching out to tenderly stop an
errant tear with the faintly abrasive pad of his thumb,
"there's nothing ironic about it. Who better to guide us
when we don't know the way than someone who's been
lost on that same path and has found his way back?"

"But that's just it," Hally exclaimed despairingly. "I
haven't found the way…"

"Yes, you have." Gently, carefully, ready to release her
if she resisted, Mike tugged her toward him, into his arms.
"You've found your way to me."

He glanced down at her lips, and they parted. "I'm going to kiss you, Halloran."

"Yes…" It was a sigh, a breath of a word that was
swallowed by the fierce possession of Mike's kiss.

Hally had barely begun to melt into it, when it ended.
Mike pulled back a little. When she opened her eyes and
blinked up at him, he said, "That was for later. For after."

"A-after?"

"Yes. After." Rising, Mike pulled her up with him.
"For after you've done what your heart is telling you to
do. After you've done what you've counseled Cory and
me to do—namely to make peace with the past, to let it
go, and begin anew."

He guided her to the door, escorted her to the car. Once
she was settled behind the wheel, he leaned in and kissed
her again. "I'd very much like to be part of that new
beginning."

Edith was out. And even though part of Hally was desperate to speak with her mother and start the healing pro-

cess, another part, the part that was emotionally drained, was grateful for the reprieve.

There was such a lot of stuff to sort through, to come to grips with. So many feelings coming at her, none of them simple. New beginnings... Yes, she wanted those. With her mother, her father and... And with Mike? Dare she risk herself to such a degree, given all the disappointments of her past?

Or was that how new beginnings were made—by going ahead full bore? By risking it all? Scary, so scary. But worth a try, just the same?

Drifting into sleep with memories of the husky murmur of Mike's voice resonating in her ear, Hally decided it just might be, at that.

The next day, Hally walked over to her mother's side of the house within minutes of coming home from school. She found Edith in her studio. Not working with glass, but sketching. Every one of Edith Halloran's pieces was an original design conceptualized and drawn by the artist herself. No two pieces were alike unless, of course, a client specifically commissioned her otherwise. Like the parishioners of St. Bartholomew's in Los Angeles, for instance. Edith had, at their request, done all of the stained-glass windows in the nave of their renovated church in an identical Medieval motif.

She preferred, however, not to work that way if she could help it. "I'm an artist, not an artisan," she liked to proclaim. Which sounded snobbish though Edith truly was anything but.

Since the studio door was ajar, Hally walked in without speaking or knocking. Edith always had the door closed when she didn't want to be disturbed. Hally suspected that the open door was her mother's way of indicating she'd welcome Hally's visit.

Edith was perched on a stool in front of her high, tilted drafting table. If she heard Hally enter, she didn't show it. She didn't look up from her work.

Hally stood by the door for long moments. Gazing at her mom, she was shocked to realize that in profile, hunched over the drawing and with the sun from the overhead skylight catching the silver in her hair, her mother looked frail. And while not exactly old, today she showed every one of her fifty-eight years.

A surge of love and tenderness brought the sting of tears to Hally's eyes. She blinked them back as she went to stand closely behind her mother and peered over her shoulder at the drawing of a delicate butterfly who had lighted on a rose.

She laid her hands on Edith's shoulders and dropped a kiss on her mother's bent head. "I love you, Momma."

She could feel the muscles tense in her mother's shoulders in that instant before, with a choked sob, Edith tossed down the stub of charcoal and spun around on the stool into Hally's embrace.

"Oh, Hally." She tightly hugged her daughter's middle and pressed her cheek to Hally's chest. "Forgive me. Please, please, forgive me."

"Shh." Hally pressed her cheek against the top of her mother's head. "There's nothing to forgive, Mom. Nothing."

"Oh, yes, there is," Edith cried vehemently, and pulled back to look beseechingly up at her daughter. "I've been a coward all these years, and a fool. I wouldn't blame you one bit if you despised me, because I truly despise myself."

"Despise you?" Hally exclaimed, bending to put her face right in front of her mother's. "Oh, Mom, never! Ever! I was hurt. I was confused. And yes, I was angry. I had to sort it all out, think it through. You know how I am..."

"Perfect is how you are," her mother proclaimed, dabbing at her eyes as Hally was doing now, too. "I don't deserve you, really I don't."

The way she said it—*muttered* it, really—and in a tone that indicated she was thoroughly upset with herself, made Hally give a watery chuckle.

"Oh, Mom…" She hugged her mother all over again. "I'm beginning to think we truly deserve each other."

They talked after that. Really talked like they hadn't done in years. Edith poured them each a glass of white wine—Semillon, nothing harsh—and they took it outside to sip in the shade of the sprawling banyan that formed a giant canopy across their entire backyard.

It seemed inevitable that, eventually, Hally would talk of Corinne. And of Michael Parker, too.

It took a couple more days for Hally to work up the courage to seek out her father. They were days that, outside of school, she spent by herself. Thinking, hoping, dreaming. Fearing. It was Saturday when she finally got in her car before she could change her mind and drove to her father's oceanfront villa.

She had debated phoning first but, in the end, had opted for the cowardly way instead. Cowardly because by not making any kind of appointment, she was free to change her mind about going through with the visit should her nerve fail her.

She would have liked to discuss it with Mike, but they hadn't spoken since that afternoon at his house, though Corinne had come up to her at school and thanked her for putting in a good word with her father about her date. She and Joey, at Hally's recommendation, along with a group of their friends, had gone to see *Eraser,* which had been totally awesome.

Hally had also debated talking to Edith about her intention to attempt a reconciliation with her father, but had discarded that notion, as well. For one thing, Edith more than had her hands full with her work and Corinne Parker's tutelage. And her head and heart were full of Bill O'Rourke.

Hally was still not entirely easy with the obviously mutual adoration this, to her, supremely unlikely couple felt for each other. But it wouldn't surprise her in the least if wedding plans were to be announced.

Of course, not being surprised by such an announcement was worlds different from being entirely happy about the event. But time enough to deal with that new wrinkle in the fabric of her life if and when the need arose.

Right now she had better decide if she wanted to cruise around the block a third time and risk being dubbed a burglar casing the affluent neighborhood, or to pull up at the curve and get the visit over with.

She decided on the latter, and got out of the car before giving herself a chance to reconsider. She didn't hesitate, forced all worry from her mind and kept her gaze fixed on the precise rows of late-blooming— *Oh, God, why am I doing this to myself?*

The silent cry caused Hally's steps to falter. And it made her wonder, Hadn't she been just fine without her dad in her life all these years?

Maybe. But only because you thought he was a villain who did you and your mother wrong.

Right. Good point. Deep breath. Head up and shoulders back. One foot in front of the other. *Peace,* she reminded herself. *You came to make peace.* Surely her father would want that, as well. He certainly had seemed to, back when Edith had been in the hospital with her lacerated hand.

Hally resolutely moved on up the path. The house in front of her was of California-Spanish architecture—white mortar walls contrasted by patches of red brick and topped by a roof of red clay tiles. A six-foot-high wall with an arched portal enclosed a slated courtyard graced by a central fountain and shaded by palms.

Standing at the wrought-iron gate beneath the portal, Hally reflected that this was the closest she had ever been to her father's home. Her heart hammered in her chest. Her palms were damp. Tentatively, she tried the gate and found it locked. Controlling the impulse to take that as a sign and to turn tail and run, Hally looked around and found the bell.

She was wiping her palm on the leg of the conservative gabardine slacks she'd chosen to wear with an equally conservative light blue silk shirt when, prior to pressing the bell, a young boy careened into the courtyard from around a corner of the house.

Hally froze. Her eyes widened. This was—had to be— her father's son. He looked too much like the childhood photos she had seen of James McKenzie to be anyone else.

Sean? Was that his name? Hally couldn't remember. Was too nervous to remember. All she could think of was that this was her little half brother.

And to wonder, with a pang of regret, if she'd been wrong in her steadfast refusal to get to know this imp who was obviously hiding from somebody. He crouched behind the fountain, caught sight of her and, giggling, put a finger to his lips for silence as Eva, James McKenzie's young wife, burst onto the scene.

"Sean McKenzie," she ordered, breathless and annoyed. "You come out this minute or you'll wish you had."

Perhaps the boy knew this to be an empty threat because he didn't budge. He did, however, slant Hally a quick glance as if to make sure he still had an audience.

As though his glance had directed his mother's, Eva's searching eyes, too, came to rest on Hally outside the gate.

"Yes?" The woman's voice had taken on a haughty

ring that immediately grated on Hally's already-sensitized nerves and made her bristle.

"I'd like to see Doctor McKenzie," she said, summoning her own coolest tone.

"I'm sorry," the woman answered quellingly. "But my husband does not see patients at his home. You'll have to make an appoint—"

"I'm not a patient." Subjected to the woman's arrogance, Hally's nervousness was fast giving way to affronted umbrage. To just assume that anyone she didn't recognize was a patient, and then to treat that assumed patient—her husband's bread and butter—in such a rude manner! "I'm his daughter."

Recalling that Morgan was no stranger here, she added, "His *other* daughter."

"Well."

Eva McKenzie's nonplussed expression gave Hally immense satisfaction. But the feeling quickly changed to bemusement as undisguised hostility narrowed Eva's eyes.

"Sean," she commanded, "get in the house. Now," she added sternly, and the boy scampered off. But not before fixing Hally with a long, half-curious, half-fearful stare.

I wonder what he's been told about me? Hally thought regretfully. Nothing good, she surmised as Eva stalked closer, her eyes glittering slits of dislike.

"You." She fairly spat the word out, stunning Hally with the venom lacing her voice. "How dare you show your face here after all you've put us through?"

"All *I've*—" Hally shook her head, hard. Surely she hadn't heard right. "What *are* you talking about? I don't even know you."

"Precisely. You don't." The woman's voice shook. "Yet all these years you've had the gall to judge me." She advanced a step, head high. "What is it you want?"

"I want to see my father." Given the woman's hostility,

Hally knew it would be futile to try to explain or reason. "Please," she added politely.

"He doesn't want to see you."

"I'd prefer to hear that from him, thank you," Hally said stiffly.

"Very well." With a chilling smile, Eva gestured with her hand. "Jim!"

Hally's eyes followed the woman's gesture and widened with shock as her father stepped out of the shadows beyond the fountain. He kept his face averted and his hands by his side, but each of his words, when he spoke, struck Hally like a physical slap across the face.

"Go home, Halloran. There's nothing here for you."

Chapter Nine

Sometime later, Hally once again found herself pulling up in front of Michael Parker's glaring pink house. Something other than a conscious decision must have guided her there. Staring blindly ahead, she just sat there. Numb.

There's nothing here for you...

Her father's words had been like the lash of a whip, flaying her raw. And they kept ringing in her ears until, with a strangled little cry, she put her hands over them, ducking her head and curling into herself. She didn't want to hear him anymore. Didn't want to think anymore, hurt anymore...

Suddenly she was frantic to get out of the car, to get to Mike. She fumbled with the door handle of the car, ground her teeth with frustration when it wouldn't cooperate. She swore when she finally thought to unlock it with fingers that shook.

She stumbled up the walk, pounded with both fists on Mike's front door, not sparing a thought to the spectacle she might be presenting to the neighbors.

"Mike!" She pressed her forehead to the age-worn wood. "Mike, please!"

"Halloran! Good *God*..." Opening the door, Mike barely had time to brace himself before Hally all but fell against him.

"Oh, Mike..."

It was a whimper that near broke his heart. Reflex had made his arms close around her. A fierce surge of possessive protectiveness now made them tighten.

"Hally. Please..." He was staggered by the desperate way she clung to him, unnerved by the waves of pain that made her tremble. "Who hurt you?" he demanded, unable to keep from pressing his lips against her temple, her forehead, the top of her hair as she burrowed into his shoulder and her nails bit into his back.

Hally couldn't answer, couldn't speak, could barely breathe past the hurt that choked her. She was shaking all over. She wanted to stop—*needed* to stop—but couldn't. She held her breath, only to have a sob painfully burst from her throat. A sob without tears.

She strained into Mike's solid strength, barely aware as he murmured reassuring words into her ear, that she was being maneuvered over to the couch. She clung to him and pulled him with her as he pressed her into the sofa's softness with gentle force.

"Hold me," she croaked past the terrible ache in her throat that even so was only a shallow imitation of the pain in her heart. "Please...just hold me..."

"I will, darling, I will." Mike soothed, stroked and petted, his lips in her hair. "Don't talk until you're ready. I'm here, sweetheart, right here."

Darling. Sweetheart... Hally's lacerated heart and wounded spirit soaked up those precious names like a healing balm.

"All I ever wanted was his love," she whispered on a

shuddering release of breath. "Nothing more. And he...he sent me away..."

What was she saying? Mike froze. Literally. His blood turned to ice. His heart stood still. *Had she come to him for solace after another man had rejected her?*

"I thought he wanted to make up," Hally went on, too wrapped up in her own misery to notice how rigid the man to whom she was clinging had become. "When I saw him at the hospital..."

So all along she'd been on the rebound. Mike felt his resentment blossoming into a full head of steam. "Hey, what is this? Do you think I've got no feelings?"

Abruptly letting her go, he shot to his feet. She'd been needy, but, it seemed, not for anything he had to offer. He glared down at her through a haze of disillusionment. "Do I look like some half-dead Dutch uncle of yours or like one of your damned girlfriends?"

Rigid with righteous outrage, he leaned down and got right in her face. "I'm a *man,* damn you."

Hally, openmouthed and thunderstruck, had no chance to acknowledge this statement of obvious fact one way or another before Mike's lips claimed hers in a harsh, almost punishing kiss. It ended as abruptly as it had begun.

"I'm a man," Mike repeated, gripping her shoulders and giving them a shake.

"I know." Hally couldn't grasp what had set Mike off. "I never—"

"That's right." He released her as roughly as he'd seized her. "You never." He towered over her like an avenging force. "Because it's all been just business with you, hasn't it? All about helping a needy student with maybe just a tad of flirtation with her schmuck of a father for vanity's sake..."

"'Schmuck of a father'?" Bewilderment about Mike's strange behavior pushed all other concerns to the back of

Hally's mind. "For heaven's sake, Mike, what's gotten into you?"

"I know I owe you, Halloran McKenzie, but..."

"You don't owe me anything."

"This is too much." His posture rigid, he strode toward the door that Hally remembered led to his bedroom. There he turned to fix her with an embittered stare. "When it's *my* love you want, maybe we can talk again. Until then, stay the hell out of my life."

Hally flinched as the slam of his door reverberated through the house. She stared at the still-quivering panel and tried to make sense of what had just occurred.

When it's my *love you want...* What did *he* mean? She'd come here for...

What *had* she come here for?

Well, certainly not for *this!* she thought with a sudden flare of indignation. Not to be yelled at, by golly. And in riddles yet!

She leaped to her feet. "Mike Parker, you come out here and explain yourself!"

His door flew open so instantly, Hally knew he'd been standing right behind it. Waiting? They glared at each other across the space separating them.

"You first," Mike snapped, crossing his arms, braced on spread legs. "This guy who upset you, who the hell is he?"

"My father." Hally took great satisfaction from the look of stupefaction on Mike's face. But a tentative gladness began to blossom inside of her, too, as it dawned on her that he must have assumed...

When it's my *love you want...* Did that mean... Had he meant...

"Michael?" She took a hesitant step toward him. "Won't you say something? Please?"

"Your father." With a groan, he subsided against the doorjamb and put a hand over his eyes. If he'd ever felt more like a horse's rear end, Mike couldn't recall. No wonder he and Cory had problems—he was the world's most insensitive jerk. And that hair-trigger temper of his... Yell first, think later, that was him. But only with the people he cared most about.

"I'm a world-class idiot. An insensitive clod..."

"Yes, you are." Hally crossed over to him, took his hand away from his face and held it between both of hers. She looked into his eyes, her tongue in her cheek because she was pretty sure now she had figured him out. "And this isn't the first time I've noticed that, either."

"I'm sorry." Mike couldn't look away from the light in her eyes, a light that warmed his blood and chased the demons and made him dare to dream again. "I'll try and do better."

"Maybe I could help you with that."

"I'm convinced that you could."

"And maybe you could help me in return."

"Help you with what? You're perfect as you are."

"Oh, Michael." How had he known that that's what she needed to hear right now more than anything? "Thank you for that."

"Thank you for *you*," Mike murmured, holding her gaze, willing her to see just how special, how precious, she had become to him. "For all you've done and all you give. Not just to Cory, but to me."

His voice roughened as emotion swelled his throat. His arms closed around Hally's body, his big hands almost covering her entire back as he urged her against him with gentle insistence. "Everything's bleak when you're not there. I try to think of ways to be together with you, ways that aren't obvious because I don't want to spook you, to scare you off. Because I'm crazy about you, Hally. Crazy *for* you. So crazy that it's turning me into a raving maniac where you are concerned. I'm jealous, I'm frustrated, and

I'm scared to death that anytime now you'll decide Cory doesn't need you anymore.

"But *I* need you, Halloran," he whispered hoarsely, all the while holding her eyes with relentless intensity. "More than anyone ever did or will again."

Hally's heart was racing and she felt dizzy in a world reduced to those wondrous emotions she read in Mike Parker's eyes—passion, desire, contrition, entreaty. And love? Surely that tender intensity couldn't be anything less.

Tell me, she thought, breathless with hope and expectation. She let her gaze caress the starkness of his somber features as it slid down to his mouth and lingered there. *Kiss me.* "Show me..."

Mike's answer to this—to Hally's unprecedented and bold invitation—was a kiss so hot and wet and greedy, it instantly turned her to mush. As his lips staked a claim, his tongue delved deep, ensnaring hers and stroking it, testing, teasing, tasting. Stoking fires too long dormant, kindling a conflagration of feelings the likes of which neither of them had ever known.

Mike had dreamed of this, had known that this was out there, that this was what it was all about—exquisite lust combined with an almost primitive possessiveness and a tenderness so fierce it rocked the very fabric of his soul.

Because he had despaired of ever finding it, he crushed her to him, his Halloran, whose size and shape filled his arms to perfection, whose pleasured little noises were music to his ears, whose pliant body together with his formed one perfect unit.

"I want you." His open mouth trailed down from her ear, leaving spots of heat where his lips had lingered.

Hally arched her neck, her hands in his hair, her hips flush against the proof of his desire. A desire that matched her own, which was as frightening in its intensity as it was exhilarating and new. She couldn't get close enough and eagerly followed suit when she felt the excitingly abrasive touch of Mike's hands against the naked skin of her back, her midriff, and—gasp—the lacy wisp of her bra.

As his thumb found her nipple and made it contract, his lips and tongue once again claimed hers. In response, Hally's fingers dug desperately into the hot skin and taut muscles of Michael's back.

They strained and clung and kissed and touched, intent on each other and their wondrous passion to the exclusion of everything else. And so they didn't hear the front door, nor Corinne and Joey's entrance.

It was the crash of the door from their exit that tore the lovers apart.

"Corinne!" After one quick exchange of mutually shocked and troubled glances, Mike let go of Hally and tore after Corinne.

He caught her on the path from his house where she was struggling to get away from Joey who was holding her by the shoulders, restraining her, talking to her.

"Cory, come inside." Mike took hold of his daughter. "Thanks, Joe. We'll see you, okay?"

Joey's self-conscious, "Sure," coincided with Corinne's near hysterical, "No! Let go of me." She struggled in earnest. "Joey!"

Mike held her, turning her toward the house with gentle force as Joey, head bent and shoulders hunched, unhappily retreated to his jalopy.

"I hate you for this," Corinne raged at Mike, more quietly now and dragging her feet.

"No, you don't." Though he said the words, Mike was far from convinced that they were true. Certainly the look of loathing his daughter sliced him was all too reminiscent of the ones he'd just begun to hope were forever a thing of the past. "We'll talk about this and you'll see—"

"No, I won't." Just inside the door, she dug in her heels, the face she turned up to Mike distorted into an ugly mask of dislike. "I've seen enough already to know that Mom was right—you *are* a womanizer!"

Hally's shocked and reproving, "Corinne!" was ignored by both father and daughter, intent as they were on their painful battle of wills.

As Corinne tore past Hally in the direction of her room, Mike bellowed an outraged, "You'll explain that remark, young lady!" and stormed after her.

Hally, worried about these two hot-tempered individuals clashing, followed, but more slowly. Her heart was heavy, for herself as well as for Mike and Corinne. The future, which, during that delirious interlude she and Mike had just shared, had seemed so full of heady promise, suddenly looked bleak again. Because they had forgotten all about Corinne.

Corinne, who had just begun to heal, and to trust. And who more than anything needed stability right now for that trust to deepen into a solid father-daughter bond.

Hally asked herself, *How could I have let myself lose sight of this, even briefly? It's what our entire relationship—hers and mine, as well as Mike's and mine—is predicated on.*

And what was this word Corinne had flung at her father? *Womanizer.* It was hardly a term that was part of a fifteen-year-old's standard vocabulary, but very much a word an embittered spouse might use in referring to a husband who was absent more than at home.

What kind of woman would use the word in front of that husband's young child, however?

The answer came swiftly and shocked Hally to the core. The same kind of woman who would discredit a child's father through silence. The way Edith had done... Every woman, it seemed, was capable of some degree of cruelty given the right circumstances.

Raised voices sounded from Corinne's room. Mike was repeating his demand for his daughter to explain herself.

Corinne was crying, "Why should I? What do you care? It's Ms. McKenzie you wanted all along, not me! It's all been an act!"

Sweet heaven, please...no. Hally leaned back against the wall, hugging herself against a surge of nausea and déjà vu. Listening, she felt as though it was herself inside that room. Her younger self, ten, fifteen years ago, ranting at her father.

And James McKenzie's protestations had sounded every bit as bewildered, hurt and defensive as Mike Parker's.

Suddenly she couldn't stand it. Couldn't tolerate history repeating itself in this way. Couldn't bear to think that another young girl should spend the next ten years or more of her life perpetuating a legacy of mistrust and misjudgment handed down from a mother who'd had her own ax to grind.

"Stop it!" She burst into the room, startling the two combatants to silence. She faced them, quivering with the force of her feelings.

"Listen to yourselves," she cried, impatient with herself because her voice cracked. "You're fighting a dead woman's fight. You're battling ghosts that have no business coming between you two in the first place. Corinne—"

She beseechingly turned to her student. "Whatever you might have overheard your mother say about your father has nothing to do with you! In an ideal world, parental issues wouldn't touch the children. We don't live in an ideal world. Adults, when they're hurting and fighting, do and say hurtful things. *Just as kids do, Corinne.*

"The trouble is—and trust me, I speak from experience—kids tend to misconstrue what is being said by adults in the heat of the moment. And so they get hurt. And they carry that hurt around with them much longer than do the adults."

Wound as tight as a top, Hally took a deep, steadying

breath. She raised her hand, palm up, when Mike opened his mouth to speak. "Please, I'm not finished."

She locked her gaze once more on Corinne's tear-filled but no-longer-quite-so-hostile one. "I sought refuge here today because, after ten years of barely speaking to my father I'd gone to him to finally make peace. And he turned me away."

She bit down hard on her lower lip, willing back tears and once again fiercely waving Michael back when he started toward her. Her gaze remained on Corinne, who had gone completely still.

"You see, I waited too long," Hally said, her throat so tight she could barely draw breath as she relived the pain of hearing her father's emotionless voice. *There's nothing here for you.*

"I never realized until now, but I had hurt him too deeply with all these years of rejection for him to forgive me when I wanted his forgiveness at last.

"Don't you do the same, Corinne," she said, and slowly backed toward the door. "Because believe me, you'll regret it. And your father—"

She looked at Mike at last, one quick, heartfelt glance. "Your father deserves better."

She turned then and, dashing tears from her eyes, hurried toward the front door.

Mike, after one hard glance at his daughter, rushed after her. "Halloran!"

Hally didn't slow; she violently shook her head, waved him back. Tears blinded her, soaked her cheeks, dripped from her jaw.

Mike caught her at the front door. Spun her around. "We're not through here," he said, hurting so much he could hardly draw breath because he knew—he *knew*—Hally wasn't hearing what he had to say. "I love you."

"Don't love me," she said, meeting his eyes with tears streaming out of hers. "Love your daughter."

"I can love you both," he said desperately.

Hally shook her head. "Not if you want Cory to love you back. Oh, Mike—" Giving in to her need to touch him, comfort him, she feathered a caress over his cheek and jaw. "Don't you see? She has got to come first in your life right now if you want her to grow into a well-adjusted human being. Whatever it takes, however long it takes, she'll never be whole until *she* feels secure in your love."

Mike captured Hally's hand and kept it pressed to his cheek. "And when will that be?"

"I don't know." Though it killed her to do it, Hally withdrew her hand and stepped back. "I wish I did."

"Will you be there...then?" Mike felt as though he were in a nightmare without quite being sure how he'd slipped into it. What had he done to his wife and child to deserve all this misery? What had he done besides work his tail off for the dream he and Becky had shared?

Though he'd come to accept that he had clung to that dream long past a time when Becky had let go of it, how had that earned him her contempt?

To call *him* a womanizer when he'd never strayed, ever. Not once. And not because he hadn't been tempted, or hadn't had offers, plenty of them. No, it just hadn't seemed right to give in to temptation when he had a wife and child who saw him too rarely and who deserved his fidelity, at least.

He had lost so much during those long, lonely years of separation—the love of his wife, the love and trust of his child.

He had wondered how, why—and now he knew. His wife had poisoned his daughter's heart and mind. And he never even knew how come.

The irony of it was that he could take it. All of it. He could live it down, concentrate on Corinne, win her back to his side. *If* he had Halloren there beside him.

"Will you be there?" he asked again, more insistently.

And died a little when she said, "I'm afraid I don't know that, either."

Hally had planned to spend most of Sunday in bed. Deep in depression, she pleaded a headache and PMS—neither entirely untrue—when Edith looked in on her on her way out to brunch and an art show with Bill.

"I don't like to leave you like this," Edith fretted, putting a cool hand against Hally's forehead the way she'd done throughout Hally's growing-up years. "You have no fever."

"I told you I didn't." Hally was in no mood to humor her mother, but also knew there was no way she would rain on Edith's happiness parade by relating all of yesterday's depressing failures.

She considered them strictly her own. Adulthood, she had learned in the course of her psychology studies, had been invented so that unresolved childhood traumas and dramas could be put in perspective and dealt with. She had waited too long to deal with a major trauma of her own. Her fault. Her problem.

"Go and have fun," she told her mother, ushering her out the door after letting Edith brew her a pot of chamomile tea. "I'll be fine. You know how I get."

"Exactly." Already on the porch, Edith turned back once more. At the bottom of the stairs stood Sergeant O'Rourke, nattily dressed in civilian slacks and a lightweight sport coat and self-consciously saluting Hally in her ratty old bathrobe.

"Put Bunny on your tummy," Edith instructed. "It'll help."

"Yes, Mother." Inwardly, Hally rolled her eyes. "Bunny" was a plush rabbit whose belly was a hot water bottle. He'd been her menstruation companion ever since she'd started "the curse" at fifteen.

Kissing her mother goodbye, it occurred to her to wonder just how much of a trauma menstruation might be for Corinne. And did the girl have a bunny, or some equally comforting facsimile? Would Mike know to offer or supply her with one, the way a mother would do?

Showering, Hally reminded herself that these days girls learned a heck of a lot in sex education classes. But...did they learn about the comfort of hot water bunnies?

Picturing Ben Franklin High School's health instructor, Louise Armstrong, conducting that particular class, Hally knew plush-animal therapy would hardly be part of the curriculum. There were simply some things that only a mother could provide.

Hally found herself desperately wishing she could be Corinne's mother. Mother substitute. Motherly friend.

She and the girl had been close to achieving the latter. But now...

Hally closed her eyes, letting her tears of regret and despair mingle with the spray of the shower. Because for all she longed to be Corinne Parker's friend, she was honest enough to admit to herself that she longed even more to be *Mike* Parker's love.

Sadly, she was also realistic enough to realize that the way things stood it seemed likely she was fated to be neither.

And was she just going to stand by and let it all slip away?

The question kindled a flicker of resentment, but she was too dispirited to stoke it into a full-fledged flame. Today, all she wanted to do was climb into a pair of sweats, lick her wounds and vegetate.

Her father, it seemed, had other ideas.

Chapter Ten

"**W**ell." Hally's initial reaction to the sight of James McKenzie at her door, was an impulse to close it in his face and tell him the same thing he had said to her, "There's nothing here for you."

She stared at the man who, dapper in tennis whites that very attractively set off his tan, nevertheless managed to look careworn and wan. And she felt a tug at her heartstrings in spite of herself.

"May I come in?" he asked.

Instead of answering, Hally just took a step back and opened the door all the way. She kept her eyes on the floor as he stepped past her, the scent of his pricey aftershave as well-loved and remembered from childhood as the smells of Christmas. She discreetly inhaled a big lungful of it and was annoyed with herself when her breath hitched.

Becoming aware that he was waiting, she finally looked up and motioned him toward the living room. He looked around as he entered it, and Hally was annoyed with herself once again because his obvious appreciation of what he saw pleased her out of all proportion.

You're all grown up now, she reminded herself, choosing a seat on a straight-backed chair. *You want peace with this man, not his approval.*

"Nice place," her father said. He sat down on the futon-style settee, but only on the edge, and dangled his hands between spread knees. "You've obviously inherited your mother's eye for style and symmetry."

"Thank you."

"You're wondering why I've come."

Hally looked down at her hands. She spoke very carefully. "Actually, I'm more curious to know why you felt it necessary yesterday to hurt me the way you did."

"I apologize for that." Her father's sigh sounded heavy; he, too, was absorbed by a study of his hands as he struggled for the words with which to explain.

At length he made a self-deprecating sound that drew Hally's gaze. "I'm not proud to admit this," he said, "but I am what's generally referred to, at least in my age group, as henpecked. It's the price, I suppose, of marrying a much younger woman. Moreover, a woman who thinks her husband's daughter shunned her and judged her and disdained her when, of course, it was me whom you judged and disdained. You were always your mother's child more than mine."

"Because Morgan was always yours."

"Perhaps." He sighed, looking grim as he seemingly studied his immaculate manicure. "It's a certainty I'm no more a match for your sister these days than I am for my wife."

He glanced up and met Hally's eyes. "You're shocked." He chuckled mirthlessly. "Most people who know me would be. *I* certainly am. But I've come to accept that it's easier, you see, to give in to Eva than to argue. Or, at least, it has been. Until now. Until yesterday."

Hally was listening to her father's humbling confession with a horrified sort of fascination. James McKenzie, the autocrat, the stern taskmaster of her childhood, the prominent physician, *henpecked?* The notion would have been laughable, hadn't her father's visible chagrin made her want to weep for him instead.

"We had a terrible row after I sent you away," he said. "I know it won't erase the hurt I inflicted, but I want you to know that I made it clear to Eva that any further interference from her in this matter will have dire consequences."

"Oh, Dad…" Hally went to the sofa and perched sideways next to him. "The last thing I want is to cause trouble between you and your wife. I came to mend fences. To tell you I was wrong…"

"That *you* were wrong?" James picked up his daughter's hand and held it. Looking down at it, he shook his head. "I can't even begin to count all the mistakes I've made where you were concerned." His eyes were tortured as he raised his head. "I wish to God I knew how to make it up to you."

"There's nothing to make up." Surprisingly, Hally realized it was true. She had truly moved beyond those hurts and slights from childhood.

"What was, was," she said. "And I've come to understand that it's not up to me to judge. Mom and I talked recently and she told me how things were, why you left. I didn't know. I used to think it was me…"

"It wasn't." James hung his head with a tired sigh. "It was me. You never knew my parents—hell, I made sure you didn't. They were drunks, both of them, and they died in some godforsaken rat's nest outside of Las Vegas when you were just five or six years old. The bottom line is, everything I knew about being a husband and a parent, I learned from them. In other words, I knew nothing. At least, nothing good. I raised myself. I fought and clawed my way out of their sewer. Everything I accomplished, I acquired through ruthless, single-minded determination. It made me a decent doctor, but a lousy husband and father.''

''Not to Morgan.''

''Morgan was different from you. Not as needy. Tougher. I didn't have to make an effort with her. I'm sorry.''

''Yes.'' Hally looked down at their joined hands through a blur of tears. ''So am I.''

James McKenzie awkwardly patted her shoulder, glanced at his watch and rose with a sigh. ''I'd like us to be friends, if we could, Halloran. Maybe have lunch once in a while, get to know each other better.''

''Sure,'' Hally said gently. She felt overwhelmingly sorry for this man who was her father, a man who, for all of his accomplishments, seemed not to have found the one thing that made it all worthwhile—true love and happiness.

At the door, she surprised him by kissing his cheek. ''Goodbye, Dad. We'll keep in touch....''

Her father's visit left her with much to reflect on. Like the messes people made of their lives. And the fact that many of these messes only became messes because people, for a variety of reasons, failed to clean them up as soon as they occurred.

The mess between herself and her father had finally been swept away. But as she put the kettle on for tea it struck her that, strangely, while it was a relief, there'd been none of the drama she'd expected their reconciliation to have, and there was none of the jubilation she had somehow imagined she'd feel.

Perhaps her unhappiness about Mike— *Whoa, girl, stop right there.*

Determined not to let herself sink back into that particular abyss, Hally snapped off the burner beneath the kettle with a decisive click. She spun away from the stove. Tea was not what she needed right now, activity was. She snatched up the bucket and headed out to her car.

Nothing like a bout of manual labor to keep a person from brooding, was what Edith liked to say. Well, the Beetle was long overdue for a wash. Hally unreeled the hose. Heck, she might even wax it, she thought, and attacked the whitewall tires with a sudsy scouring pad and an almost-fanatic zeal.

And when her thoughts stubbornly drifted back to Mike, she turned up the portable radio. But all that accomplished was to make noise. Her thoughts refused to be diverted. And her heart refused to stop aching.

Mike had left two messages on her machine so far today. Both had been brief and to the point. "I'd like to see you. We need to talk." On both of them he had sounded as unhappy as she felt. Sooner or later, she would have to take his call.

The truth was, Hally would like nothing better than to see him. And to talk. She'd drop everything and run to him right this minute if she thought it would solve anything.

The trouble was, it wouldn't. How could it? Nothing had changed overnight. Nothing would change, *could* change. Not until Corinne got a grip on who she was and what her relationship with her father was all about. These were weighty concerns for a fifteen-year-old to deal with. Especially in light of the negative campaign the girl's mother seemed to have waged.

Furious that anyone would do such a thing, Hally scrubbed at the proliferation of dead bugs that marred the VW's chrome bumper. She briefly considered being charitable and assuming the woman's illness had embittered her to the point of disregarding her child's emotional well-being. But she didn't feel charitable. She felt outraged. She felt like confronting the woman and demanding answers.

And she quivered with frustration because she'd never get the chance.

Great. Hally flung the sponge into the bucket and snatched up the hose for a final rinse. The woman was dead, leaving Mike to live with the damage. A pretty effective form of revenge, if that's what you were after....

Womanizer. Every instinct told Hally that was not something Mike Parker was or had been. Sure, she had an emotional stake. And, yes, she was probably the world's worst judge of men. But she had also worked with and observed him closely enough these past two months to have formed a pretty convincing picture of an honorable man.

So why would a wife talk about her husband in such dishonorable terms, and within hearing of their child? Perhaps to justify misdeeds of her own? They'd never know.

Dejected, Hally glanced up at the sky. Dark clouds were gathering and she knew with a sinking feeling that it was going to rain. It figured—hadn't she just washed her car?

The telephone was ringing as she came back inside. She knew it was Mike and was tempted for an instant to let the machine once again pick up the call. But then, impatient with herself, she grabbed the receiver. "Hello?"

"Halloran." His voice, the relief in it, its mellow richness, unnerved her so, she had to sit down. "Can I come over?" he asked. "Please, let me come over."

"No." She pressed two fingers to her forehead and shook her head, not meaning to sound curt, but realizing by the silence that followed that Mike had negatively interpreted her too quick, panic-induced rejoinder. The idea of another face-to-face confrontation completely unnerved her.

But she hadn't meant to hurt him. He'd already been battered enough by the women in his life. But additional heartache seemed inevitable. For both of them.

"Mike," she said, gentling her tone into one of entreaty, "what good would it do?"

"Speaking strictly for myself," Mike replied, fighting to keep a note of desperation from creeping into his voice, "it's a whole lot better than leaving things as they are." He had to see her. How could he stand not to see her? "This can't be how you want things between us to end."

"We can't end what never even started."

"It started for me." Frustration on top of the relentless certainty that his whole future was going to hell on a runaway train, had Mike's nerves strung so tight, he knew that any moment he'd snap. "And when you were in my arms, it damned well felt like it had started for you, too."

And it had. Hally blinked back tears. Dear God, yes, it had. "It was only a kiss—"

"Like hell."

Right. Hally swallowed. "Mike, I don't want to do this."

"Just like that?" Closeted in his bedroom with Corinne sulking in hers, Mike restlessly paced with his eyes on the floor, one hand rubbing at the knot of tension at the back of his neck. "I love you, dammit. Doesn't that count for anything?"

"It counts."

"But not enough to make a difference."

Hally didn't answer. What could she say—"I love you, too"? She did, God help her, she did. But if she told him, he'd be over here in a flash. And then where would his daughter be?

Mike took Hally's silence for agreement. "So that's it, then, I guess."

"I'm sorry."

"Yeah." Bitterness nearly choked him.

That's some way you have with the ladies, old bud. You made your wife hate your guts. Your daughter would rather be orphaned than have you for a dad. And the one woman you thought you might have a future with can't get away from you fast enough.

Notice she never said she loved you back. So no wonder she won't be waiting....

Well. He took a deep breath, unwilling even now to let go, to hang up and sever this final connection, yet disgusted with himself, too, for belaboring what seemed to be, at least to Hally, a dead issue. "I guess this means you, uh, won't be counseling Corinne anymore, either."

"No." Hally could barely speak for the tears burning her throat. She enunciated carefully, taking shallow breaths so as not to betray any raggedness. "Not outside of school, anyway. In any case, after, um…after yesterday, I think I'm probably the last person on earth she'd want to confide in right now. It's, uh…it'll have to be up to you now. Both of you…"

"I see." She could hardly have made it any plainer. They were through. So be it. As pride at last overrode need, Mike forced himself to retreat, to take several mental steps back and to seal his emotions away. He'd been a fool for letting them get the upper hand again in the first place.

Hadn't those final years of misery with Rebecca taught him anything? Apparently not. But he'd been slow to learn then, too. Slow to accept that he wasn't wanted when he came home on leave. Slow to realize that their dream of a horse ranch had ceased to be theirs, had become only his. Slow to believe that the girl, the woman, he'd loved since eighth grade, had found another, newer love. And in the process poisoned his daughter's mind.

Fool that he was, he'd dared to hope again. But no more. Enough. He was tired. Tired of fighting. Tired of being a supplicant.

Halloran McKenzie didn't want what he offered? Fine.

His daughter wanted to go back to Idaho? Terrific.

He was through. He was done. A job overseas sounded great. He'd look into it first thing tomorrow.

"Well." With all of his defenses firmly back in place, Mike was able to speak crisply. He was once again the cool executive who'd marched into Halloran's office. "I guess that leaves me with only one thing to say, Ms. McKenzie—thanks for everything."

"Mike, please..." Hally was shocked at the ease with which he'd slipped into the role of polite stranger. Where was the love he'd claimed to feel for her? "Can't we at least—"

"Look," Mike interrupted impatiently. What was it with women? First they tromped on every last one of your feelings in their rush to get rid of you, and then, when you took the hint, they couldn't leave well enough alone. "I'm sorry if I made you uncomfortable. Give your mother my best. You've both been great."

Oh, Michael... As the line went dead, something died inside Hally, as well. Something vital. Something precious. Something that she knew with a terrifying certainty would not allow itself to be resurrected a second time—the dream.

The dream of a man, a home, a child of her own. The dream she had forbidden herself to dream for all the years between college and now. All the years since Greg Stahl.

She put down the phone and wept for the loss.

Thanksgiving came and went. Hally spent it quietly with Edith. Bill O'Rourke was there, too, of course.

Watching her mother sneak coos and cuddles with the burly policeman was both pleasure and exquisite torture for Hally. It made her longing for Mike a physical ache. Other days she just thought about him constantly.

Many was the time that she wanted to detain Corinne after class to ask how things were going. But so far, her nerve had always failed her. Corinne had mumbled an apology right after what Hally now mentally referred to as "the incident." She'd told Hally she was sorry for the way she had acted and the things she'd said.

What she did *not* say was that she wanted Hally back in her—or her father's—life.

By and large the girl seemed well-adjusted and, outside of her flamboyant hair color and sometimes too tight sixties-and seventies-style clothes, was pretty much your average kid. She always greeted Hally upon entering and leaving the classroom. She participated in class, no longer appeared to need counseling, and completed every assignment to a fault. There was simply no reason for Hally to take her aside for questioning of any kind.

She still came to Edith's twice a week after school and every other Saturday. But Joey now drove her, and Edith, garrulous by nature and generally fond of gossip, was tight as a clam when it came to Corinne.

"The girl is a joy to tutor and guide," was the extent to which she would comment. And occasionally would proudly show off a piece or two of Corinne's work.

It was a dreary Sunday two weeks before Christmas when Edith walked in after a cursory knock. Hally was grading essays and would have preferred not to be disturbed. Not because her work required all that much quiet and concentration, but because more and more lately it suited her mood to be alone. Alone, she didn't need to put on a cheery face. Alone, she didn't need to make conversation, or smile when all she felt like doing these days was weep.

Everybody was adjusting, it seemed. Why couldn't she?

She was the one who had worried about everybody adjusting. She was the one who had counseled and cajoled and coerced the two Parkers into a workable relationship. Had they achieved that?

Outside of asking either Corinne or Mike directly, Hally had no way of knowing.

"Will you be there?" Mike had asked her on that day

of "the incident." Why, oh, why, had she said, "I don't know" when the answer should have been "Yes, yes, and yes." Because she wanted to be there. Longed to be there.

If only he would call, she'd come running. But he didn't.

"Joey deserves a lot of the credit, of course," Edith was saying.

"Hmm?" Hally blinked. As had all too often been the case of late, she'd lost track of the conversation. "Credit for what?"

"Why, Corinne, of course." Edith eyed her daughter with concern. "Are you well?"

"Of course." Hally pinched the bridge of her nose. She had a headache, but knew better than to tell Edith. "Now. Why does Joey deserve credit for Corinne?"

"Well, because he's worked wonders with her."

"In what way?"

"Well, for instance, he encourages her to apply herself, to stick with her art. She's good, but she tends to be a slacker."

"Comes with being a teenager," Hally said absently, grimly reflecting that the essay she'd gone back to grading had obviously been written by a slacker, too. One single page of drivel. She flipped it aside with a sigh.

Edith was carefully unwrapping a piece of stained glass. "Here, take a look at this." She blew at a speck of dust. "She did this. It's one part of a whole."

"Really." Intrigued, Hally accepted the heavy piece of leaded, ruby red glass. She stared at it, then frowned up at Edith. "Why, it seems to be a piece of a heart. What's it mean?"

Edith shrugged. "Corinne didn't say, and I make it a policy never to second-guess an artist's vision. It's stunning, though, isn't it?"

Stunning. Hally fingered the piece, admiring the rich colors and shadings of the glass and the way the smoothly curved side of the heart contrasted with the jagged edge on the opposite side. The latter had been cleverly cut to suggest blood dripping from an open wound. "It's really quite extraordinary."

"Yes." Edith's voice was filled with pride. "It's the best thing she's ever done. I couldn't have done better." She sighed, carefully rewrapping the piece in its bubble-wrap cocoon. "I'm really going to miss her."

"Miss her?" Hally stared at her mother, aghast. "What do you mean, miss her?"

Edith's eyes rounded. "You didn't know?"

"Didn't know what?"

"That Corinne will be staying in Idaho after the holidays."

"What?" Hally stared at her mother as though she'd suddenly sprouted horns. *But what about Mike?*

She forced the question back and tried to assume a tone of merely polite interest. "So when did all this come about?"

"I really don't know." Edith's expression made it clear that she hadn't been fooled by Hally's tone. "You know Corinne, she clams up when she's upset."

"But what is she upset about?" Hally had so many questions. Knowing her mother didn't have the answers was totally frustrating. "Having to leave? Having to stay in Idaho? What?"

"All of that, is my guess." Edith looked down at the bubble-wrapped package. "And unhappy enough to forget to take this piece home with her. I wonder if I should send it to her? Or should I go by their house?"

"I'll take it." There was no way, Hally decided, she was letting the Parkers leave town without an explanation. They owed her that much, at least.

Grim resolve firmed her tone and, incredibly, made her feel better than she had in weeks as she said, "Trust me, Mother, I'll take care of it."

Edith smiled. "I was hoping you would."

Chapter Eleven

Hally had hardly been able to sleep. Here, finally, a legitimate reason to approach Corinne in a personal, nonacademic, but also nonthreatening way after class had been handed to her. Returning the girl's property, what could be more innocuous than that? If, in the course of the ensuing conversation, there should arise an opportunity for Hally to ask a few questions…well, it wouldn't be anything planned and overt then, would it?

Having lived the scenario in her mind all night long, the letdown at finding Corinne absent from school was twice as—no, a thousand times more crushing. Especially since, as homeroom teacher and Corinne's assigned advisor, Hally also received a notice from the principal's office stating that Corinne would not be returning to class.

Hally couldn't have said how she got through the day. Probably the only thing that kept her focused was her increasingly fierce determination to drive to the Parkers home the minute school was out. Whatever was going on, Hally intended to find out.

And if Michael Parker was around, she intended to give him a piece of her mind.

After all, the least the man could have done, given the energy she had expended on him and his daughter, was to keep her abreast of his plans. Regarding Corinne and—yes, darn it—regarding his own life, too!

Pulling up to the curb in front of the awful pink house, Hally immediately noted two things—Mike's car was parked in its usual spot. And Pamela Swigert, dressed to the nines, was emerging from her house next door, clinging to the arm of a visibly well-heeled older man.

So, at least Mike hadn't been squiring the nubile Pam around.

Torn between relief and exasperation at the way her mind worked, Hally picked her handbag and Corinne's carefully wrapped broken heart off the seat and got out of the car. She stood, hesitating, looking at the house for a moment, trying to pick up clues, see beyond the drawn blinds, get past feeling like an unwelcome intruder.

Only her refusal to remain forever locked in a limbo of uncertainty made her toss her head and march up the walk to the door. Only simple stubbornness made her knock.

"Oh. Hi." She hadn't been prepared to be faced by an older version of Mike. His father. Had to be. Was she ready for this? She was *not* ready for this. She stammered, "I, uh, I hope I'm not disturbing you, but—"

"You'd be Ms. McKenzie." The older Parker stuck out his hand and hauled her inside. "Recognize ya from the pictures."

Pictures?

"Mike's not here right now, but— Iris!" He smiled at Hally, who was wishing now she'd called first. "We got company!"

"Company? Now who in the world..." A tiny birdlike woman fluttered into the room. She peered nearsightedly at Hally. "Well, my goodness gracious..."

"It's Ms. McKenzie, dear," Mike's father explained, steering the flustered Hally to the sofa. "You recall—"

"Well, of course I do." Iris Parker made an impatient shooing motion with her hand at her husband while fixing Hally in a curious stare that was not entirely friendly. Hally tried to keep in mind that anyone who owned, and appreciated, several of her mother's creations—and who also happened to be the mother of a pretty wonderful man— couldn't be all bad, but it was an uphill battle. Especially when the woman remarked, "You're prettier in person, aren't you?"

Hally was saved from having to come up with a suitable rejoinder by Corinne. "I told you, Gramma, she'd just got rescued from drowning."

"By you, as I recall," Hally said, gratefully turning to where Corinne stood in the living room doorway. Their eyes held for several heartbeats. Hally detected a sheen of tears glazing Corinne's.

She turned to the elder Parkers. "It's a pleasure meeting you both, and I, uh, I won't intrude for very long…"

"No intrusion," Mike's father interjected.

Liking him, Hally gave him a smile as she said, "Could I possibly have a moment alone with Corinne?"

"Why sure you can," Mike's father said resolutely when it seemed his wife hesitated with a dubious expression. "You're her teacher, aren't you? Take all the time you need," he added, glancing crossly at his reluctant spouse as he hustled her out of the room.

"Gramma saw the picture of you and Dad," Corinne explained, eyes still brimming and visibly ill at ease. Hally couldn't tell if it was about her grandmother's attitude, the photo, or just in general. "It's the one where Dad had his arms around you."

"Oh." Hally's heart contracted as she recalled how safe and warm she'd felt snuggled against Mike after her watery mishap. "That one. Joey took it, didn't he?"

"Uh-huh." Corinne sank down next to Hally on the edge of the sofa and looked away as she furtively wiped at her eyes only to immediately swivel toward her with a heartrending sob. "Oh, Ms. McKenzie..."

"What? Oh, baby." Instantly concerned, Hally pulled the young girl's unresisting body into her arms, babbling questions without really expecting answers. "What is it? Won't you tell me? Where is your father? What can I do?"

"I hate my life!" The wail came from very deep down. "I hate myself!"

"Oh, hush, now. You don't mean that...." Meaningless words. Of *course*, Corinne meant it. She was miserable and saying exactly what Hally wished she herself were still young enough to simply blurt out.

"I've been so m-mean," Corinne sobbed. "And h-he...he's so unhappy..."

Corinne wiped at her nose with the back of her hand, sniffling as the tears continued to course down her face.

Hally dug into her pocket and came up with a somewhat rumpled but unused tissue that she wordlessly pressed into the girl's hand.

"It makes him look and act angry all the time." Corinne noisily blew her nose. "Just like after Mom died, only worse. He never laughs or even smiles anymore."

The tears fell anew as she wailed, "And it's all my fault. I've been so mean. I wanted him all to myself. And I was jealous. And when he told me he...w-was in love with you, he—"

"He—" Hally cleared a lump from her throat. "He told you..."

"Yeah. That he loves you." Corinne paused to blow her nose again, while Hally hugged to her heart the bittersweet knowledge that Mike loved her as she loved him. She was filled with tenderness and compassion for the young girl's misery, and pretty close to tears herself. Inhaling a shaky breath, she fumbled for words of reassurance.

But Corinne forestalled her with a halting, "H-he also said, though, that his f-feelings for you wouldn't...you know, change anything. Between him and me, I mean. H-he s-said that, um, I'm all that counts, that being a real dad, and loving me, was the most important thing in the world to him right now..."

"And it *is*," Hally exclaimed fervently, her need to reassure this child overriding her own sense of loss. "Oh, Cory, the last thing in the world I'd ever want to do is come between you and your dad."

"But, Ms. McKenzie..." Corinne caught Hally's hand and clutched it as she lifted tear-swamped, pleading eyes. "I really want you to."

"You really want me to do *what?*" Hally asked, bewildered. "I don't understand..."

Cory visibly swallowed; her eyes continued to implore. "I want you to marry my dad," she blurted, her desperate grip on Hally's hand all but cutting off circulation. "Oh, please, Ms. McKenzie, marry him. Make him stay here..."

"But—"

"Oh, please. *Please.* I don't want us to move back to Idaho. Please?"

Us to move back to Idaho? Not just the girl, but Mike, too? Hally sat bolt upright. "Is *that* what your father is planning?"

"Ye-ees," Cory cried. "He already told the school and Gramps and Gramma are taking me with them tomorrow. Oh, Ms. McKenzie, I'll hate it there now. I know I will. Gramma hates my hair and clothes. And I wouldn't see Joey anymore. Or you. And Edith. And...I'm so sorry, Ms. McKenzie."

"I know you are." More than a little sorry herself, about a whole lot of things, Hally soothingly rubbed the girl's back.

"Have you tried telling your father all that?" she finally asked.

"Nu-uh." Corinne once again pulled back, this time using the hem of her blouse to mop up her tears.

Since Hally didn't have another tissue to offer, she simply sat by. "Why not?" she asked.

"I don't know." Corinne shook her bent head, twisting the soggy shirttail into a tight spiral. "I was scared to, I guess, after...you know. I'd been so mean to him about...about you and all."

"Where is he now?" Hally smoothed a hank of magenta hair away from Corinne's mottled cheek.

"On a business trip. To some oil place I can't even pronounce the name of and he's coming straight from there to Idaho. F-for Christmas." Her eyes beseeched again. "So will you?"

"Oh, Cory..." Only too aware what Corinne was asking, Hally shook her head with a sad little smile. "I wish it were that simple. If it were up to me... Well, it isn't. And anyway, I..."

Finding it difficult to bare her fragile and vulnerable hopes and emotions, Hally faltered. But then she realized that it was crucial she be as open as Cory had been.

She took a deep breath. It audibly shivered on the way out. "The trouble is, you're not the only one who hurt your father, Corinne. I hurt him, too, by thinking that only I knew what was best and how the future should be."

Gently disentangling her fingers from Cory's, Hally stood up and walked to the window. Dusk was falling. Multicolored outdoor Christmas lights winked and flashed. Their very cheeriness made her sadness increase.

"Like you," she said, "I've been miserable and unhappy, which is always what happens when we do something hurtful to the people we...care about. I regretted the, uh, things I said to him and I came over here today because in my heart of hearts I was hoping..."

Faltering, she turned back to Corinne with a helpless shrug.

The girl's eyes shone. "You love him," she exclaimed, jumping to her feet and running over to clutch Hally's hand. "Don't you?"

"Oh, yes," Hally said softly. "I love him."

"I'm glad," Corinne whispered, startling Hally by pressing an impulsive kiss onto Hally's cheek. "'Cause then I guess you won't mind that I put a piece of this heart I made into his suitcase."

The heart. With everything that had transpired, Hally had forgotten all about the package she'd brought. She went back to the sofa and took the wrapped piece of glass out of her handbag. "One like this?"

"Yeah, kind'a." Corinne quickly ducked her head. "I meant this piece for you, though."

"For me?"

"Uh-huh."

Corinne's cheeks were crimson and she wouldn't lift her head. "I was going to send you a letter, too, to, uh, apologize and, um, explain. But now, well..."

She ventured a smile that twisted, and captured, Hally's marshmallow heart with its sweetness. "Now you're here and I won't need to since I already told you most of what I was gonna write."

Her smile became abashed. "Like, you know, that I'm sorry and all."

"Oh, Cory." Hally went to the girl and gave her a hug. "I know. And I understand, believe me." Afraid that she might be making Corinne uncomfortable by continuing to hold her close, she pulled back. "Tell me, though, what you want those pieces to mean."

Corinne flushed more deeply and her chin quivered, but she kept eyes that brimmed again fixed on Hally's. "I made them to show that I know I'm responsible for breaking all of our hearts—"

She stubbornly shook her head at Hally's appalled, "No, Cory. It wasn't just you." She went on, undeterred, though her voice quaked. "But that we can mend them if we all come together. I was hoping…"

She took Hally's hand, and in a tentative voice that grew increasingly animated as Hally's eyes began to glow, she related the scenario she'd envisioned while crafting the heart.

After a week in Azerbaijan, Mike knew three things. One, that life on an oil rig would never again be for him even if he hadn't already made up his mind to other pursuits like running to ground one particular, stubborn female and making her marry him. And even if he hadn't found his daughter's touching artwork—a fractured glass piece of what was clearly a heart—in his suitcase after arriving in Baku. It was winter, it was cold, and on the oil rigs floating offshore in the Caspian Sea, it was noisy, it was grimy and it was lonesome as hell.

He saw it on the faces of the other Americans and Europeans—engineers, geologists, mechanics and roustabouts—all of whom sent there by their respective companies to help Azerbaijan to develop their oil fields. He saw loneliness, homesickness, all the same ills and emotional deprivations he himself had suffered during those many long years abroad.

No, thank you, Charlie. And never again. He was out of here the minute this little fact-finding junket was concluded.

The second thing he knew now—again thanks to that mysterious piece of stained-glass art—was that at long last his daughter loved him. Why else would she have sent anything along with him on this trip at all, least of all something she had created?

And maybe it was that crazy shard of red glass that had led him to his third revelation—namely that Cory would be able to handle it when he told her what he needed to do, which was to follow his own heart to Halloran McKenzie's doorstep.

Because come hell or high water, Halloran McKenzie, his counselor, his friend, his *love*, would become Halloran Parker even if he had to bodily drag her to the altar. He loved her. And she, by gosh, loved him.

First chance he got, he'd make her see that.

It was a long way from Baku, Azerbaijan, via Moscow, Russia, to Boise, U.S.A. A long way in every respect—culturally, geographically and logistically. The combination of flights, stopovers and grueling hours required to bring Mike back to rural Idaho in time for Christmas was daunting, but only an act of God could have prevented him from making that trip.

His reunion with Corinne was everything he'd dreamed it would be. Her joy and her fervent hugs went a long way toward eradicating the bitter memories of past, less rewarding homecomings.

Christmas was chock-full of traditions, food and family as both his folks as well as Rebecca's went all out in their effort to lure them back into the fold. Back home, where he belonged.

But Marble Ridge wasn't home for Mike anymore. Long Beach, California, was. Or, more precisely, anywhere Hally lived, was.

With all the holiday hubbub, it was several days before the chance to discuss this with Cory presented itself. And then it was she who opened the door.

"Everybody here thinks I'm weird," she lamented, after dragging him away from the family for a walk in the snow. "Both grandmas are always picking on my hair and my clothes, and my friends aren't really my friends anymore. I miss Joey. And..." She threw him an uncertain look. "And I, um, really miss Ms. McKenzie."

Mike's heart slammed into his ribs as he stopped in his tracks and searched his daughter's face. "You do?"

Eyes wide with expectation and hope, she nodded. "Uh-huh."

"Oh, baby," Mike said, his voice rough from the wealth of emotions that filled him as he hugged his child to his chest. "If you knew how much I needed to hear you say that."

After a long hug during which neither of them spoke, Corinne leaned back and peered into Mike's face. "You gonna marry her?"

He dropped a kiss on her nose. "You gonna mind?"

"Only if I can't be a bridesmaid."

They grinned at each other. And then, as though on cue, linked hands and marched for the house, loudly singing, "Californ-ya here we come...."

He'd been an idiot to go along with Corinne's hare-brained scheme. But she had been so excited, so adamant.

Scowling, Mike paced the living room of his Long Beach house, realigned a chair he'd just moments before placed at an angle, then stopped at the coffee table to scowl down at his leaded, stained-glass section of heart.

Straightening, he glanced at the ormolu clock on one of the half-empty bookshelves. Ten past two. She was ten minutes late. She wasn't going to show. As he'd known she wouldn't. He should have gone to get her. To make her listen. To plead, and beg. To—

He spun toward the rap on the door. It was tentative but it reverberated through Mike's emotionally heightened hearing like a sonic boom. His heart lurched into action after weeks of hanging like a lump of lead in his chest.

She had come. She was here. But she had to knock once again before Mike could make his feet carry him to the door. He opened it slowly, almost reluctantly. What if it wasn't her? What if it was some peddler, or—God forbid because he was in no mood to deal with her now—Pam Swigert?

But, no—her he would have smelled by now. The thought made a grin tug at the corners of his mouth.

And that was the first thing Hally saw when Mike opened the door all the way.

That grin. That endearing, lopsided, heart-stopping grin. It made her knees go weak and her pulses race. And it kept her frozen on the threshold because she was suddenly scared to death.

He didn't look heartbroken. He didn't look nervous. He looked like a man who hadn't a care in the world. While she, on the other hand...

"You look wonderful, Halloran." Mike congratulated himself on the steadiness of his voice. For a moment there, struck dumb by the lovely picture Hally made in a fuzzy pink sweater and hip-molding slacks that weren't really white, he was afraid his voice would crack when he spoke. "Come in."

"I'm sorry I'm late." Mike's scent embraced Hally as she moved past him into the house. She'd know it anywhere—clean male, starched linen and crisp aftershave. "My car..."

"Another flat tire?"

"No." Their eyes met and the memory of the flat she'd had the night of the concert riot hovered between them.

"The ignition," Hally said breathlessly as their eye contact lengthened and the air between them grew heated and thick. "It didn't want to—"

"Well, I do." As his forceful and unexpected announcement startled her into openmouthed silence, Mike took immediate advantage of it by yanking her into his arms and covering her lips with his own.

"I want to so much, it's tearing me apart," he said hoarsely before kissing Hally again. Longer, hotter, the kiss betrayed a level of desperation that was every bit as deep as Hally's and which annihilated the walls she'd erected around her heart prior to coming over here today.

She'd been afraid. She hadn't known what to expect. She had hurt him so much. And she'd cautioned herself that a fifteen-year-old girl's fantasy didn't necessarily translate into a real-life dream come true just because said fifteen-year-old wished for it with all her heart.

And so it was heaven and more to be in Mike's arms and to know that dreams could come true, after all.

"I can't believe you're really here," Mike murmured, raining kisses over her face, her throat, her eyes, her nose, while his hands roamed feverishly, tracing her form, lingering here, tantalizing there. "I've missed you. Thought I'd lost you…"

His voice cracked. He closed his eyes and pressed his forehead to hers. "Sweet heaven, Halloran, I've been in hell."

"Me, too. Oh, Mike, me, too." An overwhelming tenderness momentarily overrode passion as Hally's hands rose to Mike's face. As her eyes caressed his every feature, so her fingers gently stroked and learned him. His cheeks, slightly abrasive in a thoroughly manly way. His lips, finely etched, soft to the touch for all they could look so severe. A nose that was interesting rather than straight, and the back of his neck where his hair was soft and touched the collar of his shirt.

Her hands slid higher then, to the back of his head, and as passion once more asserted itself, she raised herself up a bit while urging him forward to give him her lips, already eagerly parted.

"I love you," she whispered. And when, breathless, they pulled apart and gazed into each other's eyes, she told him again. "I love you."

"That day…" Mike began, needing to know. "Did you…"

"Yes," Hally said. "I already loved you even then. I

couldn't tell you, though. I didn't dare. Because I didn't want to be responsible for any more trouble between you and Corinne.''

"If I'd known, I'd never have let you get away.'' Mike's arms tightened around her, pulling her even closer as though he feared that even now she might slip from his grip and be lost to him forever. "We would've worked it out…''

"No.'' Hally nuzzled the palm with which he was cupping her cheek. "It had to be this way. It had to come from Corinne. That heart…''

Her eyes filled. "I brought my half with me. Do you have yours ready?''

"Of course.'' Mike nodded toward the table. "Right there, as per Corinne's instructions. Is it two-thirty yet?''

He took his hand from Hally's face and turned his wrist. "Hey, just about.'' He kissed Hally's nose. "Much as I hate to postpone this—'' he kissed her again, on the mouth and more lingeringly ''—till later, we'd better do as we were asked and put the two pieces together. Just one more thing, though, before we do.''

His eyes turned somber and deep. "I love you, Halloran. And I fully intend to make you mine.''

"Too late,'' she murmured against his lips. "I'm yours already, in every way but one.''

"I'm looking forward to changing that to 'in every way, period.'''

"So am I.'' They lingered over another kiss, but mindful of the time and their expected visitor, they kept their passion banked with promises of later. They pulled reluctantly apart as the front door opened and Corinne's head appeared in the opening.

"Well?'' she asked with a heartbreaking look of uncertainty that changed into a huge grin at Mike's and Hally's thumbs-up.

"Cool.'' She all but skipped inside, closed the door and

immediately complained after a quick glance at the table, "You guys haven't done the heart yet."

"We were just about to," Hally said, flushing beneath Cory's pleased but knowing expression as she carefully unwrapped her piece of glass.

Her shoulder touched Mike's as they bent over the table together while she arranged her piece adjacent to his.

"But..." Her eyes flew to Corinne's at the other side of the table. "I thought you said they'd fit. That the heart would be complete."

"And it is. Now." With a flourish, Cory produced a narrow sliver of stained glass and fitted it into the gap between theirs. "There," she said with evident satisfaction. She raised shining eyes to the adults. "See?"

"Yes," Hally breathed, clasping Mike's hand while he reached across the table and took hold of Corinne's. "Oh, yes, I see."

And as together they looked down at the table, they did indeed see Corinne's vision—three parts of a heart that made up a whole. But they also saw a future that was full of love, sharing and promise.

* * * * *

Daniel MacGregor is at it again...

New York Times bestselling author

NORA ROBERTS

introduces us to a new generation of MacGregors
as the lovable patriarch of the illustrious MacGregor
clan plays matchmaker again, this time to his three
gorgeous granddaughters in

THE MacGREGOR BRIDES

From Silhouette Books

Don't miss this brand-new continuation of Nora Roberts's
enormously popular *MacGregor* miniseries.

Available November 1997 at your favorite retail outlet.

Take 4 bestselling love stories FREE

Plus get a FREE surprise gift!

Special Limited-time Offer

Mail to Silhouette Reader Service™

3010 Walden Avenue
P.O. Box 1867
Buffalo, N.Y. 14240-1867

YES! Please send me 4 free Silhouette Romance™ novels and my free surprise gift. Then send me 6 brand-new novels every month, which I will receive months before they appear in bookstores. Bill me at the low price of $2.67 each plus 25¢ delivery and applicable sales tax, if any.* That's the complete price and a savings of over 10% off the cover prices—quite a bargain! I understand that accepting the books and gift places me under no obligation ever to buy any books. I can always return a shipment and cancel at any time. Even if I never buy another book from Silhouette, the 4 free books and the surprise gift are mine to keep forever.

215 BPA A3UT

Name	(PLEASE PRINT)	
Address		Apt. No.
City	State	Zip

This offer is limited to one order per household and not valid to present Silhouette Romance™ subscribers. *Terms and prices are subject to change without notice. Sales tax applicable in N.Y.

USROM-696   ©1990 Harlequin Enterprises Limited

Bundles of Joy

Babies have a way of bringing out the love in everyone's hearts! And Silhouette Romance is delighted to present you with three wonderful new love stories.

October:
DADDY WOKE UP MARRIED by Julianna Morris (SR#1252)
Emily married handsome Nick Carleton temporarily to give her unborn child a name. Then a tumble off the roof left this amnesiac daddy-to-be thinking lovely Emily was his *real* wife, and was she enjoying it! But what would happen when Nick regained his memory?

December:
THE BABY CAME C.O.D. by Marie Ferrarella (SR#1264)
(Two Halves of a Whole)
Tycoon Evan Quartermain found a *baby* in his office—with a note saying the adorable little girl was his! Luckily next-door neighbor and pretty single mom Claire was glad to help out, and soon Evan was forgoing corporate takeovers in favor of baby rattles and long, sultry nights with the beautiful Claire!

February:
Silhouette Romance is pleased to present ON BABY PATROL by **Sharon DeVita,** (SR#1276), which is also the first of her new *Lullabies and Love* series. A legendary cradle brings the three rugged Sullivan brothers unexpected love, fatherhood and family.

Don't miss these adorable Bundles of Joy, only from
Silhouette ROMANCE™

As seen on TV!
Free Gift Offer

With a Free Gift proof-of-purchase from any Silhouette® book,
you can receive a beautiful cubic zirconia pendant.

This gorgeous marquise-shaped stone is a genuine cubic
zirconia—accented by an 18" gold tone necklace.

(Approximate retail value $19.95)

Send for yours today...
compliments of ▼ *Silhouette*®
TM

To receive your free gift, a cubic zirconia pendant, send us one original proof-of-
purchase, photocopies not accepted, from the back of any Silhouette Romance™,
Silhouette Desire®, Silhouette Special Edition®, Silhouette Intimate Moments®
or Silhouette Yours Truly™ title available at your favorite retail outlet, together with
the Free Gift Certificate, plus a check or money order for $1.65 U.S./$2.15 CAN. (do
not send cash) to cover postage and handling, payable to Silhouette Free Gift Offer.
We will send you the specified gift. Allow 6 to 8 weeks for delivery. Offer good until
December 31, 1997, or while quantities last. Offer valid in the U.S. and Canada only.

Free Gift Certificate

Name: _____

Address: _____

City: _____ State/Province: _____ Zip/Postal Code: _____

Mail this certificate, one proof-of-purchase and a check or money order for postage
and handling to: SILHOUETTE FREE GIFT OFFER 1997. In the U.S.: 3010 Walden
Avenue, P.O. Box 9077, Buffalo NY 14269-9077. In Canada: P.O. Box 613, Fort Erie,
Ontario L2Z 5X3.

FREE GIFT OFFER   084-KFD
ONE PROOF-OF-PURCHASE
To collect your fabulous FREE GIFT, a cubic zirconia pendant, you must include this
original proof-of-purchase for each gift with the properly completed Free Gift Certificate.

084-KFDR

SILHOUETTE WOMEN KNOW ROMANCE WHEN THEY SEE IT.

And they'll see it on **ROMANCE CLASSICS**, the new 24-hour TV channel devoted to romantic movies and original programs like the special **Romantically Speaking—Harlequin™ Goes Prime Time.**

Romantically Speaking—Harlequin™ Goes Prime Time introduces you to many of your favorite romance authors in a program developed exclusively for Harlequin® and Silhouette® readers.

Watch for **Romantically Speaking—Harlequin™ Goes Prime Time** beginning in the summer of 1997.

If you're not receiving ROMANCE CLASSICS, call your local cable operator or satellite provider and ask for it today!

Escape to the network of your dreams.

See Ingrid Bergman and Gregory Peck in *Spellbound* **on Romance Classics.**

MEN!

The good ones aren't hard to find—they're right here in Silhouette Romance!

MAN: Rick McBride, Dedicated Police Officer
MOTTO: "I always get the bad guy, but no good woman will ever get me!"

Find out how Rick gets tamed in Phyllis Halldorson's
THE LAWMAN'S LEGACY. (October 1997)

MAN: Tucker Haynes, Undercover Investigator
MOTTO: "I'll protect a lady in need until the danger ends, but I'll protect my heart forever."

Meet the woman who shatters this
gruff guy's walls in Laura Anthony's
THE STRANGER'S SURPRISE. (November 1997)

MAN: Eric Bishop, The Ultimate Lone Wolf
MOTTO: "I'm back in town to find my lost memories, *not* to make new ones."

Discover what secrets—and romance—are in store
when this loner comes home in Elizabeth August's
PATERNAL INSTINCTS. (December 1997)

We've handpicked the strongest, bravest, sexiest heroes yet! Don't miss these exciting books from

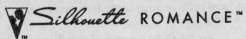

Available at your favorite retail outlet.

You've been waiting for him all your life....
Now your Prince has finally arrived!

In fact, *three* handsome princes
are coming your way in

ROYAL WEDDINGS

A delightful new miniseries by **LISA KAYE LAUREL**
about three bachelor princes who find happily-ever-
after with three small-town women!

Coming in September 1997—THE PRINCE'S BRIDE

Crown Prince Erik Anders would do anything for his
country—even plan a pretend marriage to his lovely
castle caretaker. But could he convince the king, and
the rest of the world, that his proposal was real—before
his cool heart melted for his small-town "bride"?

Coming in November 1997—THE PRINCE'S BABY

Irresistible Prince Whit Anders was shocked to
discover that the summer romance he'd had years
ago had resulted in a very royal baby! Now that
pretty Drew Davis's secret was out, could her kiss
turn the sexy prince into a full-time dad?

**Look for prince number three in the exciting
conclusion to ROYAL WEDDINGS,
coming in 1998—only from**

Silhouette ROMANCE™

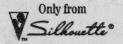